G.H.

D1061620

Ч

Ambush Creek

OTHER SAGEBRUSH LARGE PRINT WESTERNS BY
LEWIS B. PATTEN

Feud at Chimney Rock

No God in Saguaro

Ambush Creek

LEWIS B. PATTEN

Sagebrush
Large Print Westerns

Library of Congress Cataloging in Publication Data

Patten, Lewis B.
    Ambush creek / Lewis B. Patten.

Library of Congress Cataloging in Publication data was not available in time for the printing of this book. Please write or call the publisher to be sent CIP data for this title by mail or by fax.

Cataloguing in Publication Data is available from the British Library and the National Library of Australia.

Sagebrush Large Print Westerns are published in the United States and Canada by Thomas T. Beeler, Publisher, Box 659, Hampton Falls, New Hampshire 03844-0659. ISBN 1-57490-126-5

Published in the United Kingdom, Eire, and the Republic of South Africa by Isis Publishing Ltd, 7 Centremead, Osney Mead, Oxford OX2 0ES England. ISBN 0-7531-5885-X

Published in Australia and New Zealand by Australian Large Print Audio & Video Pty Ltd, 17 Mohr Street, Tullamarine, Victoria, 3043, Australia. ISBN 1-86340-755-3

Manufactured in the United States of America by BookCrafters, Inc.

Ambush Creek

CHAPTER 1

CONVERGING THEY CAME, FROM MANY DIRECTIONS along many streams, riding their horses in the swift-running, icy water and leaving no trail. With this task done, they would, with luck, return in the same way, faceless and unknown.

Behind them the sky was a flawless blue and the sun beat warmly down on the thawing, running land, bringing early spring flowers poking through the rich black soil, bringing a sheen of green to the long, south-facing mountain slopes.

Snow, drifted and dirty, still lay on the north slopes, in the ravines, and along the creeks. But far to the east the pass was open and the coach was going out, carrying the winter-earned riches of the gold camp on Ute Creek, the camp called Unionville. Phil Coyne had brought the news only yesterday, the news he had stayed all winter in Unionville to obtain.

Reaching the road at the bridge over Crazy Woman Creek, Major Jefferson Crawford drew his horse to a halt and stared west along the rutted, muddy road. It held no coach tracks yet. The stage wasn't due for at least an hour if Coyne's story was accurate and Crawford had no reason to think that it was not. He withdrew a cigar from his pocket and tucked it under his left arm while he trimmed the end off carefully with his pocketknife. Finished, he put it into his mouth, lighted it, and puffed luxuriously. With the cigar clamped tightly between his teeth, he withdrew the Navy Colt's revolver from his belt and checked its loads. Satisfied, he returned it to his belt.

1

He began looking for the others now, climbing his horse out of the creek bottom and up atop a low knoll so that he could see. He saw Hobo Jennings half a mile away, coming down the east fork of Crazy Woman Creek and, a mile farther east, saw another man riding in the bottom of Grizzly Creek, a man who, from this distance, looked like Phil Coyne.

Crawford was a tall, whip-lean man in his early fifties. He wore a neatly trimmed, pointed beard and a moustache, both of which were liberally sprinkled with gray, as was his hair. He wore a wide-brimmed gray hat with the insignia of the Confederate Army pinned in front. Beneath a flowing gray cape, he wore the uniform of the Confederacy and the gold oak-leaf insignia of his rank.

Hobo Jennings came splashing along the creek, saw the major, and rode toward him in disapproving silence. He raised a hand in a half-hearted salute, in itself a concession to the major's former rank but by its sloppiness expressing his disdain for the military. He was a heavily bearded man in miner's clothes, with dirt under his fingernails and in the creases of his neck. His eyes were blue and as sharp as a ledge of polished winter ice. They were about all he showed the world of himself and if you wanted to evaluate him all you had to go by were his eyes and his voice, which may have been the way he wanted it. Right now he said plaintively, "Jesus Christ, Crawford, why'nt you bring a trumpeter? They're goin' to know you the minute they see that uniform."

"They'll know all of us. They'll know why we want the gold and what we intend to do with it."

"Then you don't mean to leave no one alive. Is that what you're tellin' me?"

2

"Not necessarily. Perhaps I want the people of Unionville to know who got their gold. Perhaps I'd like them to come after it. Then we would settle once and for all whether this park will belong to the Union or the Confederacy." He stared haughtily at Jennings for a moment and then went on. "This is war. This is war just as much as Bull Run or Antietam or Pea Ridge, and our job is to get that gold to the Confederacy. No matter who gets hurt. No matter what." He flung the cape back deliberately, exposing the stump of his left arm as he did. He said, "I gave the bastards this arm at Bull Run"—he looked down at the stump bitterly, almost with revulsion—"and now I'm half a man. Do you think I'm going to worry about the men on that stage? I don't give a damn whether they live or die. What happens depends on them."

"Your sayin' this is war don't make it that. We ain't soldiers and we sure as hell ain't goin' to be treated like soldiers if we get caught."

"If you are afraid there will be no need for you to stay."

Jennings scowled at him. "Biggety when you get that goddam uniform on, ain't you? But don't talk to me like that. You ain't a major and I ain't a buck private. I'm here because I want them boys in Georgia to have food an' guns an' the clothes they need. I'm goin' to stay an' do my bit to help them get the guns. I'll shoot anybody on the stage that shoots at me, but don't tell me this is a battle in the war. It ain't. Nothin' anybody says will make it one."

Crawford glared at him and started to speak. He changed his mind when Coyne rode out of the water and climbed the knoll toward the pair.

Coyne was a small, scrawny man in his thirties. He

3

had a birdlike quickness of gesture about him, and small, bright brown eyes above an unshaven face. His nose was red; it was always red, whether from an excess of alcohol or the sun, or both, Crawford didn't know. He carried a double-barreled shotgun that looked like a cannon in his hands. He was riding a powerful black gelding that he seemed to have trouble holding still. He nodded at the two. "None of the others get here yet?"

Crawford pulled his big gold watch from his pocket and flipped open the hunting case. Inside there was a picture—cracked and browned now with age—of a pretty, fragile-looking woman. "There's still three quarters of an hour before the stage is due," he said. "They'll be along."

He glanced northward toward the tall, brooding, snow-covered hills. Some of those dark mountains had snow on them all year round, above the fringe of timber that dressed the peaks like demure green skirts. The high range was thirty miles away and the descent to this park was made by a series of stair-stepping smaller peaks until the terrain became nearly flat down here in the park.

The park itself spread southward for another thirty miles. East and west it was twenty miles across, cut with clear streams, with low, timbered ridges and knolls, and lush with wild prairie hay. A paradise for game. A bonanza for gold-seeking men—in places at least. In places like Unionville. It was almost as though, thought Crawford, God himself had blessed the Union cause, giving the abolitionists at Unionville all the gold, the Southerners in the valley of Grizzly Creek nothing. Nothing but the land and grass.

He saw another figure winding down Grizzly Creek, and two more coming along a fork of Grizzly Creek that

4

had no name. Coming up Crazy Woman Creek from the east, he saw three more. That made nine, and nine would be enough if the others didn't ever get here. He had no idea how many would be on the stage, how many guarding it. A driver and guard on the seat, perhaps. A couple more inside. Possibly an outrider or two. He didn't think there'd be more than six. Nobody would be expecting a military force to attack and capture it and it ought to be easy enough. All they had to do was shoot one of the lead horses and bring him down. That would stop the stage and those defending it would be in the open. The attackers would be concealed.

The ethics of ambushing the stage didn't bother Major Crawford. There were no ethics in war. Quantrill hadn't been thinking of ethics when he rode in and burned the town of Lawrence, Kansas. A military commander worth his salt planned his campaigns so that he would win—with as little loss to his own troops as possible while inflicting as great a loss as possible on the enemy. That was the way wars were fought and this would be no exception to the rule.

The others straggled up, each glancing sharply at Crawford and at his uniform. There was disapproval on the faces of all of them, and it was plain they thought, as Jennings did, that this was an unnecessarily flamboyant touch, a needless risk placed upon them all to satisfy Crawford's vanity.

Crawford looked at his watch again, then glanced along the road toward Unionville, snapping the hunting case of his watch shut and returning it to his pocket. There would be no dust to announce the approach of the stage. He glanced quickly around at the terrain, his eyes sharpening, his mouth thinning speculatively.

He rode down off the knoll to the bridge, then back

5

along the road toward Unionville for a couple of hundred yards. Turning his head, he shouted, "McCurdy! Stocker! Lead your horses up the creek bottom until they're out of sight. Tie them and come back here on foot!"

He watched while they complied. The mud was deep on the road and beside it, and they floundered helplessly. Crawford waited patiently until they reached him. He waved his right hand at a cut left by the scraper making the fills for the bridge approaches. "Get down in there out of sight. Don't call to them and don't order them to stop. Just shoot one of the lead horses in the neck."

"And then what? Looks like we'll be takin' all their fire."

Crawford shook his head. "We'll be mounted, the rest of us. As soon as we hear your shots, we'll attack."

McCurdy was a stocky man, gray-bearded and blue-eyed. His skin had a ruddy color to it and there was a strange instability about his eyes, as though wildness hovered close to the surface needing only the slightest of excuses to erupt. His voice was hoarse and rasping when he spoke. "What else, Crawford? What are we supposed to do after we drop the horse?"

Crawford stared at him with harsh contempt. "Why McCurdy, I shouldn't think you would need to ask me that. The men on that coach will be armed. They will be shooting at us as we come out from beneath the bridge. I should think you would return their fire if they do."

"They'll slaughter us."

Crawford was briefly silent, his glance searing McCurdy. Then he said, "You may go back home if you wish. You may quit if you are afraid."

A dark flush stained McCurdy's face. For an instant

6

his eyes flared with wildness, a flame leaping high. He blinked and looked at the ground, fists clenching at his sides.

Crawford stared down at him. McCurdy was dangerous. He recognized that fact. He was unstable and dangerous and no man would ever know exactly what he was going to do. Sullenly McCurdy followed Stocker, a yellow-haired young giant in his early twenties, toward the cut left in the gravel by the scraper and its team. They settled themselves in the cut, only their rifle muzzles visible. There was a bit of stirring there, and sound, as they scraped mud off their boots. Then they were still.

Crawford rode back to the bridge. Too late, he realized his horse had left tracks in the muddy road. Also visible were the boot tracks of McCurdy and Stocker. He felt a little foolish forgetting about tracks, felt his face grow hot with embarrassment. He hoped none of the others would notice the oversight. He hoped the stagecoach driver wouldn't see the tracks. If he did, he'd be on guard an instant sooner than he would otherwise.

He waved the others down beneath the bridge. They were not completely concealed, he realized, but they would not be seen until the coach was about a hundred yards away and anyway, it would be better to have them seen than to hide them well up the creek. Time was of the essence here. A few minutes, or even seconds, might spell the difference between failure and success.

He could see Luke Hamidy's face from where he sat. And the rump of Hamidy's horse beyond. Hamidy had a young face, pallid and clean-shaven. A bony face with eyes deep set in cavernous sockets. Hamidy was even more dangerous than McCurdy, but in a different way.

7

Hamidy would do nothing wildly or recklessly. But there was something lacking in Luke. Crawford didn't know exactly what it was. Conscience maybe. Maybe the brake that held most people back was absent in Luke Hamidy. He'd been in the Confederate Army but had been discharged. Not for wounds. There had been a rumor about the torture of some Union prisoners, but that probably wasn't true Still, it was odd, a young man like that being discharged. A veteran, and the South in such desperate need of men.

With time getting short, the old nervousness that always came over Crawford just before a battle began to put tremors into his arms and legs. He gripped the horse's barrel with his knees, so that no one would see. He held the stump of his left arm close against his body, and clenched the hand that held the reins.

But if there was nervousness, there was eagerness as well. There was a rush of blood, a surge of new life pounding through his head. His eyes brightened, and his mouth firmed, turning slightly downward at the corners. His head assumed a new tilt, and beneath him even the horse seemed to sense the change in him.

He thought he heard something in the distance, the rattle of tug chains or doubletree, and an instant later caught a faint and distant shout. He called, "They're coming, McCurdy. Get one of the lead horses, now. We're counting on you."

He turned his horse and put him down the steep, rocky bank into the bed of the stream. He rode to where the others sat their fidgeting horses nervously. He smiled a tight, cold smile. He said, "Just think of all that goddam Union gold and what it's going to buy for the armies of the Confederacy."

Looking them over, he knew that they would fight.

8

They would do whatever had to be done. They weren't brigands risking themselves for loot and personal gain. They were soldiers, fighting for a cause. This place might be a thousand miles from the war raging in the South, but wherever there were men from the Southern states, the Confederacy lived and breathed. Here, he thought, it was beginning to stir restlessly.

CHAPTER 2

THE HORSES DRAWING THE COACH WERE RUNNING when they came into sight. Running, and the driver half standing on the box, whip in hand, yelling at them.

Great gobs of mud were flung up from their hooves, pelting the coach, sometimes pelting the lower legs of the driver and the guard. They were lathered, these teams, on their necks and where the harness strapping rubbed. The lead animals had a froth at their mouths.,

A driver and a guard. That was all Crawford saw at first. The coach was coming at him head-on and he couldn't tell whether anyone was inside the thing or not.

But he could see the outriders, riding far enough back so that they wouldn't catch any of the high-flung gobs of mud. Back about fifty feet, but that was enough. God knew that would help.

Crawford saw the driver stand straight up, saw him haul back on the reins with both hands as he saw the tracks that Crawford and the other two had left in the muddy road. But he hadn't succeeded in slowing the teams before McCurdy and Stocker stood up in the cut and opened fire on the near lead horse.

9

The horse collapsed, and the others piled up on him, and an instant after that the coach piled up on them. But not before one of the men inside the coach got off a shot, a bullet that caught Stocker in the chest and drove him back with the force of a mule's kicking hoof. He disappeared into the cut, leaving McCurdy standing there, a smoking rifle in his hands.

Crawford already had his spurs raking his horse's sides, already was leaping him up out of the bank of the creek, loosing a shot at the stagecoach guard an instant before the pile-up catapulted the man forward off the box and into the melee of frantically fighting horses and tangled harness and singletrees.

Crawford's horse reared. He was forced to seize the reins in his right hand, the same hand in which he held the gun, yanking them from beneath the stump of his left arm where he had put them so that his right would be free to shoot.

The horse floundered in the mud and nearly fell, but Crawford held on to reins and gun and when the horse dropped to all four feet, wrapped them around the saddle horn and raised his gun to shoot again.

The outriders had pulled their plunging horses up just behind the coach, which was tipping, now, two of its wheels raising up off the ground. "The damn thing's going over," thought Crawford, as he snapped a shot at one of the mounted guards, at the only one of the two that he could see.

The bullet struck the man squarely in the throat, and his front was instantly drenched with blood. He fell from his saddle, but his foot did not come clear of the stirrup. Maddened and terrified by the noise and the hot smell of blood, the horse bolted, dragging the dead outrider behind, kicking out at him every second or third jump, trying to get him loose.

There was a lot of shooting behind Crawford now, and as the coach went over onto its side, the second outrider became visible beyond. Immediately, he drew a volley of fire from the six men behind Crawford, and was literally driven backward out of his saddle. He hit the muddy road on his back and did not move afterward. His horse, stung by one of the bullets, bucked away after the other one.

The coach skidded ten or fifteen feet sideways in the mud, tilting off the road, nearly standing on its top when it came to rest. Crawford could see the passengers struggling to get out the window. Bullets kept striking the mud in front of the window they were trying to come through, showering them with mud, driving them out the other way.

McCurdy stood up in the gravel cut. Hamidy had ridden around on the far side of the road. The two fired like executioners, dropping everyone that came crawling out.

Something about Hamidy's face, about his eyes, held Crawford's stare as though he had been mesmerized. Hamidy wasn't doing this because it had to be done; he was enjoying it. His eyes blazed, flamed in his cavernous eye sockets. His mouth was a tight, thin line, yet it held the slightest of smiles, ugly and obscene.

Crawford literally yanked his glance away from Hamidy's face. The horses were still struggling, three of them. Two of the wheels on the overturned coach were spinning. A quarter-mile away the horse that had dragged the dead outrider away was still running and the other horse had almost caught up, having stopped bucking and started to run. Crawford couldn't see any of the passengers' bodies, but he knew they all were dead.

Hamidy and McCurdy had stopped shooting. That was how he knew.

Crawford yelled, "Get the gold! Look sharp, now. It won't all be in one place!"

A strongbox had fallen from the boot beneath the driver's box and now lay overturned in the mud at the side of the road. Suitcases and valises and boxes had tumbled out of the covered boot at the rear of the coach. Unwilling to get his boots muddy if it wasn't necessary, Crawford forced his horse close enough to the stage so that he could look down inside of it.

A woman was lying there, a young woman in her mid-twenties, a pretty woman. He stared closely at her, looking for signs of life, but there were none, no pulse in her pale white throat, no rise and fall of her breasts. But her eyes were open. Her eyes were open and staring up at him. He felt an uncomfortable, ugly chill run along his spine.

He reined his horse away and rounded the rear of the capsized coach. Hobo Jennings and Phil Coyne had dismounted and were rummaging through the luggage that had tumbled from the boot. Crawford rode down off the road to where Hamidy and McCurdy were, thinking, too late, that there might have been other outriders who had fallen behind He yelled, "Two or three of you scout back down the road!" and watched Fall and Goldsmith and Stebbins trot their horses down the road toward Unionville. He must be getting old, he thought. He wouldn't have made that mistake two years ago when he'd been on active duty. That kind of carelessness could cost him his life. It could cost him unnecessary casualties. It could mean defeat. And it wasn't the first mistake he had made today. There had been the tracks left in the mud before the coach arrived. He had made

12

two mistakes already and he couldn't afford any more.

There were three bodies in the ditch beside the road, spilled there by Hamidy's and McCurdy's bullets as they came crawling out of the coach. All three were dead.

He sat his horse, looking around, feeling himself relax for the first time today, feeling a warmth of satisfaction that nearly chased away the ugly chill caused by sight of the dead woman in the coach. The job was done. It had been done successfully.

A shout went up from Coyne, who had found a canvas sack so heavy he could not lift it by himself. Almost immediately afterward, a bullet clanged against the strongbox lock, breaking it, and the top was yanked open to reveal leather sacks stacked like cordwood inside of it. Crawford bawled, "Each man take six sacks, three to each saddlebag! Then we will see how many more are left."

The men began to load their saddlebags with gold. McCurdy went back beneath the bridge and got his own and Stocker's horses. He led them to where Stocker's body lay, then called to Hamidy. "Gimme a hand here, Luke."

Between them, McCurdy and Hamidy lifted Stocker's body and laid it face down across his saddle. McCurdy lashed it down while Hamidy held the horse. After that, McCurdy led the two horses to the strongbox and carefully loaded the leather pouches into the saddlebags, six to a horse, three on each side.

No one mentioned the dead woman inside the coach. There was little talking among the men. They were subdued, shocked by the slaughter here. They finished loading gold and one called to Crawford, "Nine sacks left, Major."

"Hand them up to me." He guided his horse to where the strongbox lay, making a rapid calculation in his mind. The sacks ought to weigh fifteen pounds apiece. Six sacks to a man was about ninety pounds. Nine men with ninety pounds each was over eight hundred pounds. That would be over a quarter of a million dollars in gold. A fortune. A sizable contribution to the Confederacy and God knew it would help. It would save a lot of lives, maybe a hundred times as many as had been taken here today.

That was the way to look at it, Crawford thought. There was no use letting himself dwell on that dead woman inside the coach. Yet her face and her open, staring eyes remained in his thoughts, like a picture etched indelibly. He couldn't rid himself of his feeling of guilt and regret that something had been done that could never be undone. But she hadn't been killed deliberately. She couldn't have been killed deliberately because she'd never gotten out of the coach. She had either been killed when the coach overturned or had caught a stray bullet meant for someone else.

The gold was all loaded now and the men were looking expectantly at him. Crawford said, "Rifle the bodies. Take everything that has any value. We want this to look like an ordinary robbery."

Hobo Jennings said, "I thought you wanted 'em to know it was us."

Crawford realized he was thinking about the dead woman in the stage. He didn't want anyone connecting him with that. He said shortly, "I changed my mind. The gold is more important than a showdown with the Unionists."

No one challenged his explanation and no one mentioned the dead woman inside the coach. Neither did anyone go inside to search her for valuables. They searched the dead men outside the coach halfheartedly. When they had finished, and had mounted, Crawford drew his revolver from his belt and put a bullet into the head of each wounded horse.

Raising his arm, then, he waved them away toward home. He took the reins out from beneath the stump of his left arm where he had tucked them just before he shot the horses and guided his horse down into the bed of Crazy Woman Creek. He forced the animal into the water. Riding this way, paying no attention to the others, he headed away toward home.

There should have been more elation in him than there was. He had engineered a raid that would give the Confederacy over a quarter of a million dollars in gold. He had succeeded spectacularly, and had lost only one of his men. No one else had even sustained a wound.

But all he could think of was that pretty young woman lying dead. All he could see in his mind was her face, and her open, staring eyes.

Unionville sat scattered on both sides of its single street, a collection of log and frame shacks, some with stone fireplaces and chimneys, these having been built of round, stream-polished rocks taken out of Ute Creek which ran at right angles to the main street at its lower end. There were even a few dirty white canvas tents along the creek bank, and one miner, who had a squaw, lived in a buffalo-hide tepee she had brought with her when she left her Cheyenne village on the plain two hundred miles away.

The Stars and Stripes flew on a pole over the town hall, a log building no more prepossessing than the rest. Adjoining the town hall was the sheriff's office and his jail, also built of logs. Laws were passed in the town hall; they were enforced in the adjoining building. Tom Condon did the enforcing, being the duly elected sheriff of Lincoln County, which encompassed the entire park and some of the high peaks lying to the north of it.

Condon was a young man, still in his early thirties, but there was a calm steadiness about his eyes, a firm patience about his mouth usually not present in men his age. He had fought in the Union Army for almost a year and had been discharged after he had been wounded in the chest. It did not affect him much, that wound, only when he was forced to some violent physical exertion. Then his breath would get short, his face pale, and he would begin to gasp almost helplessly.

He did not, therefore, permit himself much violent exercise. If he was called upon to subdue a quarrelsome drunk, his methods were so quick and so violently effective that he did not have time to get short of breath.

It was at noon of the day following the departure of the first stagecoach out of Unionville that year that he saw the horse come walking into town. The reins were dragging and the horse's head was turned so that he would not step on them. The saddle he wore was empty, but Condon recognized it instantly. It belonged to Nate Widemeier, who had ridden behind the stage as guard.

As soon as he recognized the saddle, Condon began to walk swiftly toward the horse. Fifty feet away he began to talk soothingly, and twenty feet away slowed his pace drastically so that he would not frighten the animal. The horse fidgeted and danced away a few steps, then stopped and stood still until Condon caught the reins.

He stroked the horse's neck as his eyes examined the saddle. There was only one dried, brownish spot of

16

blood on it, partially smeared, but it told Condon what he had to know. The stage had been attacked. Nate Widemeier had been shot out of his saddle and was probably dead. The gold had been stolen. And Lucy . . .

Turning, forgetting his war wound and his tendency to shortness of breath, he ran for the livery stable, leading Widemeier's horse. It was not far, less than a hundred yards, but there was a tightness in Condon's chest when he arrived.

No one was in the stable and that suited him. He yanked off the saddle and carried it to the tackroom. He tossed it down where it would not be noticeable, picked up his own saddle and carried it out into the cavernous livery barn.

He led Widemeier's horse to the rear and turned him into the corral. Returning, he got his own strong gray gelding out of his stall and led him, bridled, to the front of the stable where he saddled him. He mounted and rode out, turning immediately at the corner of the livery barn and leaving town by way of the creek bed where he was not likely to be seen.

He wanted to know exactly what had happened to the stage and he wanted to know immediately. But he didn't want a mob along with him, and that's what he'd have if the people of Unionville suspected they had lost their gold.

CHAPTER 3

THE ROAD WAS MUDDY, DEEPLY RUTTED BY THE wheels of the stagecoach, pocked with the hoofprints of the horses drawing it, scattered with clods flung up by those hooves. Condon pushed the gray horse hard, alternating between a lope and a steady, bone-jolting trot. Occasionally the horse floundered almost helplessly at some spot where the mud was very soft, but Condon did not let up on him. Urgency was pushing him now, urgency that had stark terror in it. Lucy had been on that stage, headed east to Denver for her wedding dress. She was to become Mrs. Tom Condon two months from now.

At the very least, even if she wasn't hurt, she'd had to spend a cold and miserable night out there in the park. The stagecoach must have been disabled, or it would have returned to Unionville.

At the worst. . . Condon shook his head angrily, trying to drive away the spot of cold that was growing in his chest. Lucy could be dead.

He'd been a fool to let her go on the first stagecoach out of the park this year, a coach carrying all that gold. But she had been so excited, so anxious. . . And it wasn't as though the coach hadn't had plenty of guards. There had been two men on the box, three more inside the coach. There had been two outriders. All had been hand-picked and heavily armed. All had possessed a stake in the load the coach was carrying. Suddenly he raked his horse's sides with his spurs, forcing him to a reckless speed, forcing him to hold that speed even when his neck began to fleck with foam.

Overhead the sky was blue and out of the south blew a warm and thawing wind. Puffy clouds drifted across the sky, sometimes covering the sun briefly and throwing a shadow across the greening land. These shadows made a spotted pattern across the vast and open park, visible whenever the road climbed some ridge or minor elevation.

Once Condon saw a bunch of elk skylined on a ridge. Several times he drove deer out of some brush-grown creek bottom, and watched them bound out of sight over a brushy ridge. At last, straight ahead, he saw vultures circling in the sky.

The icy spot spread now until it filled his chest. Fear made his breath short, his breathing fast. There was no anger in him yet, and wouldn't be until he knew. But terror drove him on, drove his spurs mercilessly into his horse's sides.

He didn't see it until he was three hundred yards away, and when he did see it, he felt as a man must feel at the moment of his death. The coach was off the road, tilted almost onto its top, its four wheels sticking up into the air.

The coach horses were a pile of dead and bloating flesh. A couple of buzzards perched on one of the horses, tearing, tearing at the red and bloody meat.

Condon yanked out his revolver and fired unthinkingly. The buzzards squawked and rose, flapping violently, into the air. Fighting off disgust and nausea, Condon flung himself from his horse, sliding in the mud, running toward the coach.

He had not missed the body of Nate Widemeier lying there, his throat ripped open by a bullet, black now with blood that had dried. He had not missed the body of Milt Snyder, literally riddled a few yards away.

But they were dead and beyond his help. Inside the coach. . .

He reached it, knelt, and peered inside. And suddenly his heart seemed to stop.

Numb with shock, he hung there to the side of the coach, his knuckles white with the desperate tightness of

19

his grip. She was beyond his help. Oh God!

Condon had seen death before. He had seen the slaughter of a rebel cannonball bursting in men closely packed. But this was ten times worse because this was not even war. This was murder—for profit—for a few bags of yellow dust. This was cold-blooded and merciless. There had been no fight here, only slaughter, planned and deliberate.

He rose and pushed himself away from the coach. He felt numb and dazed. He shook his head, trying to force himself to think, trying to force a return of sanity, even though there could be none until this insanity was punished and avenged.

Slowly, slowly his numb mind began to think again. To think, even though doing so was painful in the extreme. He was sheriff of this county and upon him fell the responsibility of bringing these murderers to justice. There were tracks in the road between here and the bridge, tracks deeply indented and plain, both of horses and of men. Carefully, in order to smudge none of them, he walked slowly toward the bridge, studying the ground as he did.

He saw where two of the party had left the road and walked to the cut left by the scraper and team. Leaving the road, he walked to that cut.

Here they had crouched, and here they had scraped mud from their boots while they waited for the arrival of the stage. Here, too, he found a spot of blood and knew that one of them had been hit.

He left the cut and returned to the side of the road. Slowly, studying the ground as he went, he approached the bridge and followed the tracks under it.

Here he found more tracks, pounded into the creek bank, poorly defined and not clear enough to identify.

20

But he could make an estimate as to the number involved in the raid. Between seven and ten. It had been a cold-blooded ambush, the two in the cut opening fire first, the others riding out from beneath the bridge and finishing off the stagecoach guards still left alive.

He returned to his horse, mounted, and began a careful circle of the area. It was a wide circle at first, a half mile in diameter, and it turned up not a single track. It was as though the raiders had disappeared into the air.

But the circle crossed several streams, Grizzly Creek and its unnamed fork, Crazy Woman Creek and the east fork of Crazy Woman Creek. The raiders had come and gone in these four streams, their tracks washed out and gone. They were nameless and anonymous but even so, Condon knew, if not who they were, at least from whence they came. From that damned rebel settlement at the head of Grizzly Creek.

He cocked his head and squinted at the sun. He turned and stared at the stage with shock still in his eyes. It seemed indecent to leave her thus, but it was better than trying to take her in on his horse. Turning his horse he dug spurs into him and rode away in the direction he had come. The buzzards circled lower and lower in the sky until at last two of them alighted with a squawk on the bloody carcass of a horse.

Condon's horse was worn out from the hard ride getting here, but he kept him at a trot all the way back to Unionville in spite of that. Arriving in mid-afternoon, he went at once to the town hall and began to ring the bell. The way he felt he didn't care what happened to that bunch of rebels at the head of Grizzly Creek. He didn't care if the men of Unionville declared war on them.

But when he saw them approaching, some running, some walking, all showing worry and concern, he knew

21

he couldn't let it happen. Not here. Not to the people of Unionville or even to those of the rebel settlement. He was here to enforce the law and keep the peace. It was his job and his alone to find the men responsible for the stagecoach attack and to recover the gold if possible.

He waited until thirty or forty men and women had gathered in the street. Then he went outside. He raised his voice and yelled, "The stagecoach has been attacked. The gold . . ."

His voice was drowned out as they all began to shout at once. He roared, "Damn it, listen to me! The gold is gone. The men are dead!"

Someone shouted, "How about Lucy? Is she . . . ?"

He said, "She's dead too," and suddenly became aware that tears were running down his cheeks.

A man roared, "Get your horses, everybody! We'll get the bastards that done it! We'll get our gold back too!"

Immediately there was a roar of voices in the street. Condon listened for an instant, tempted to let them go, tempted to let them have their revenge. But only a handful of men had participated in the robbery. At the settlement on Grizzly Creek there were fifty people, forty or more of whom were innocent. He bawled, "No! Hold it, every damn one of you! Nobody's going anywhere. There isn't a track half a mile away from the place. There isn't a trail you can follow."

"Then what're you going to do?"

"I'll find tracks. I'll find the men. But I won't have twenty or thirty hotheads breathin' down my neck while I do. I won't have anybody telling me every move. Now get a wagon and a bunch of men and go on out there for the bodies. I want 'em brought back to town and given a decent burial. I want the stagecoach righted and brought

22

back in. I want those dead horses dragged off the road. Then I want you to stay here and wait until you hear from me."

"You know who did it, Tom?"

He shook his head.

"But you've got an idea. That it?"

Again he shook his head. He felt irritable now, edgy and mean. He yelled, "I'll find them, but I'm going to do it my way. If any of you got any different ideas, let's hear them now!"

There was still some yelling in the crowd, but it was not continuous anymore. And there was some grumbling, not in the front ranks but at the rear. Condon held them with his stare, challenging, daring any one of them to grumble to his face.

Slowly, reluctantly, they began to melt away. They were as shocked as he had been at first. They needed time to get used to it. But when they had, they would begin to plan and nothing on earth, not Tom Condon, not fifty like him would be able to hold them back. They had lost their gold, representing a winter's work to most of them, more to some who had been hoarding it. Worse, they had lost it to a bunch of rebels, a fact most of them would realize soon. If they suspected that it was going to help the rebel cause . . .

Condon knew he had not much time. If he failed to recover the gold and bring the culprits in, war would come to this high and remote park. There would be a battle here, a battle that would not stop until all on one side or the other were dead.

Eight were already dead, perhaps nine if the one whose blood he'd found had died. Eight, including Lucy Wiley. Condon's face twisted suddenly. Lucy dead. Lucy, who would not smile at him again, nor touch his

23

face gently with her hand. Lucy . . . God!

He turned away and hurried to his office door. He went inside and stood there, fists clenched at his sides, his whole body trembling.

He didn't know whether or not he could forestall a bloodbath here. He wasn't even sure he wanted to. The men who had attacked the stage deserved to die if anyone ever had. Once he'd found out who they were, he might even execute them himself.

He had stopped the people of Unionville, temporarily at least, but he had done so from habit, and because his own numbness and shock were still so strong he could not think clearly or logically.

He didn't know what he'd do when the shock wore away and the pain set in. He might do anything. But right now he'd do what he'd sworn to do when he took the sheriff's oath. He'd try and keep the peace.

He went out, untied the gray and led him toward the livery barn. There was utter confusion in the street, people running this way and that. On the veranda of the mercantile store Nate Widemeier's wife sat in a chair, her strong, gaunt face buried in her hands, weeping almost soundlessly, rocking, rocking, rocking. . .

Condon reached the livery barn, anger growing in him now. The horror of war had been brought here and he was angry at the uselessness of it. This was Colorado, in Union territory. Nothing could change that fact.

He guessed they hadn't really meant to change that fact. They had only wanted the gold for the Confederacy. To help prolong its life. Perhaps hoping to help the doomed cause win.

But they were butchers, and the stagecoach guards and Lucy had died in vain. A hundred times that much

24

gold couldn't save the Confederacy. Not now. Condon knew that, even if the rebels on Grizzly Creek did not.

CHAPTER 4

THE LIVERY BARN WAS A SHAMBLES, FULL OF MEN catching horses, saddling, yelling. Len Purdue, the town's part-time undertaker, was hitching up the hearse, which was kept inside the stable to protect it from the weather.

Condon watched a moment, then took the rope from his saddle and walked toward the corral at the rear.

He pushed into the corral, stood a moment beside the gate watching the horses stream past as they were driven around the corral in a galloping circle by the yelling men waiting to make a catch. He saw a likely looking bay he knew and flipped out his loop. It settled over the bay's head and tightened as Condon laid back against it. The horse stopped and the others streamed away from him, leaving him there alone.

Condon walked to him, coiling the rope as he did. The other horses, coming around again, streamed past on both sides and when they had gone on, he led the bay to the gate, through it, and back into the livery barn. He replaced the catch rope with a bridle and changed his saddle from the gray to the bay. Mounting, he rode out into the rutted, muddy street.

Piled-up ice and unmelted snow still lay on the north side of the livery barn but on the south side the grass was turning green and was already two or three inches high. Condon headed north out of town. He caught himself thinking he ought to stop and tell Lucy good-bye before he left. He stopped that thought before it was complete, an expression of anguish touching and narrowing his eyes. It would be a long time before he'd be able to think of Lucy without hurting when he did. He touched spurs to the bay's sides and lifted him to a steady, rocking lope.

This way, he went out of Unionville and headed north. Back on Union Avenue, the town's main street, a group of townspeople watched him go, some with sympathy, some with respect, some with doubt that he could do this by himself.

He wasn't aware of them, indeed was not aware of his surroundings at all. He gave the horse his head, frowning, a faraway look in his eyes.

He was thinking of Lucy, not in terms of a great love lost but in terms of the little things he had shared with her.

Like last winter when he'd asked her to marry him. He'd blurted it out standing at her door in a howling blizzard when the temperature was twenty-five below. She'd stood motionless in the doorway, staring at him, and he'd stood motionless on the porch staring at her, waiting for her answer and knowing he'd picked a hell of a poor time and place to ask. The wind had blown past her, depositing snow halfway across the room. Suddenly they both had realized how ridiculous it was to stand so dumbly in the howling wind, and they had both begun to laugh. He'd crowded in, closing the door and taking her in his arms. The laughing had stopped as suddenly as it began, before something overpowering and wonderful. She had never told him yes, he thought now. She'd never had to put her answer into words. It had been a thing both of them knew without needing

26

any words.

But he remembered now her warmth, and her light fragrance, and the laughter in her eyes and the softness of her mouth. He remembered walking down to the schoolhouse after the children had all gone home, remembered sitting cramped at one of the children's desks waiting for her to get through with her work so he could walk her home.

He remembered the golden leaves on the aspens and on the willows along the stream. He remembered the incredible blue of the sky, with its puffy, drifting clouds. He remembered the smell of woodsmoke drifting to them on the crisp fall breeze, and he remembered the way her hair had smelled when he held her and buried his face in it.

And finally he remembered the way she had looked when he had seen her last, awkwardly sprawled where she had been tossed by the overturning of the coach, her eyes open, but dull and changed and dead. He remembered that and he looked ahead with smoldering anger in his eyes that would not soon go away. Men were going to die on Grizzly Creek. The men who had killed Lucy were going to die. But first he had to know who they were. He had to go among these people who believed so fanatically in the Southern cause, with them knowing he was a Yankee who had fought on the Union side, with them knowing who he was and why he was in their midst.

Nor did he have much time. Two days and two nights at most. Then, if he had not returned, the men of Unionville would come looking for him. They would come like an army and they'd be prepared for war. They would attack the settlement on Grizzly Creek and wipe it out. Or be wiped out themselves in an ambush laid for them.

It was late afternoon. The sun hovered halfway down the sky. A haze hung over the vast and open park, hiding the peaks to east and west and south. Rivulets of melting snow out of the high country swelled the streams to roaring cataracts and flooded the low-lying areas of the park.

Condon cut straight across country, using Johnson's Peak as his guide. He splashed across meadows an inch deep with water, forded flooding streams. He climbed dry south-facing slopes, and put his plunging horse through drifts still four feet deep on their timbered north sides.

As he traveled, he became more intent. His eyes narrowed, sweeping restlessly back and forth over the country lying ahead of him. They would not, perhaps, expect him to come alone. They would be expecting a force from Unionville. In spite of their precautions, in spite of the fact they had left no trail, they'd be expecting a force from Unionville. And they'd be ready. They'd be ready for that force, waiting and dug in.

At sundown, he caught a flash of sun on metal half a mile ahead of him. He continued, without pause, without noticeable hesitation. But now he was looking for a way out, for a way around, for some cover that would hide him long enough to change his course and avoid those he knew were waiting there for him.

He had no way of knowing what they would do. They might open fire the instant he came in range, dump him from his saddle, and leave him for the buzzards. They might stop him and question him before they murdered him. Since he was only one, they might even let him pass, claiming to have no knowledge of the wrecked and looted stage. But he didn't intend to take the chance if it

28

could be helped.

There was no cover, and no way he could escape. So he drew his horse to an immediate halt, dismounted, and lifted the horse's right rear hoof to look at it. After that, he made a show of digging for his pocket knife, of digging at the mud-caked frog of the horse's hoof as though searching for a stone. All the while he watched the land ahead out of the corner of his eye, stalling, waiting for the sun's last light to fade from the high clouds overhead and for the curtain of dusk to descend and give him a chance to get away, to get around the men waiting there for him.

It was hard to be so deliberate, so roundabout when he knew those men were the same ones who had looted the stage, who had killed Lucy and the stagecoach driver and the guards. Yet he had to be realistic. He was only one. He could not take on half a dozen or a dozen men by himself. Trying would accomplish nothing. He'd only succeed in getting himself killed.

Light continued to fade. But suddenly he caught movement where he had seen the sunlight flash and he knew he had run out of time.

Instantly he mounted and galloped away at right angles to the course he had been traveling. He didn't have to look to know they were thundering in pursuit.

As he rode, he cursed softly to himself. He would have given a great deal to have been able to elude them and slip back, to listen to their talk and thus find out who they were. But there'd be no chance for anything like that now. He'd be lucky just to get away.

He had obtained an advantage, though. They would be leaving trails from here to their homes after they gave up trying to catch him in the dark. Tomorrow those trails could be followed out, and they would lead him, one by one, to the men who had participated in the looting of the stage.

A few shots racketed, but none of the bullets came close to him. At last all light had faded from the sky.

When it was completely dark, he turned at right angles to the course he had been traveling, not back toward Unionville as they might expect, but away from it. He slowed his horse to a walk, dropped into a stream bed heavily lined with scrub willow, and drew the animal to a halt. Leaning forward he stroked the horse's muzzle with his hand, ready to clamp that hand over his nostrils if the bay smelled the horses of the pursuit.

He heard a few scattered shouts, some hard-pounding hooves, and then silence as they gradually diminished and faded away. Still he made no move, waiting, and after nearly five minutes of this, was rewarded by the sound of two more sets of horses' hooves pounding away in the direction all the others had gone. He smiled grimly to himself, giving them silent credit for being smart enough to leave two men behind in case he had stopped somewhere nearby and hidden out.

He dismounted as soon as the sound of hooves had died away and unsaddled. He staked out in a little grassy clearing across the stream, then returned to his saddle. He untied his blanket roll, wrapped himself in his blanket, and lay down to sleep. He felt satisfied with what he had accomplished so far. He had ridden into their ambush without being caught; he had drawn them into a chase and had eluded them. Most important of all, he now had trails to follow, trails that had to belong to men involved in the looting of the stage.

He closed his eyes. The time was short, but tomorrow he could begin following out those trails.

He did not sleep at once. His mind kept seeing the

stagecoach as he had seen it first, resting on its top with its four wheels sticking up into the air. He kept seeing the piled-up dead horses, torn open and bloody, the buzzards rising, flapping, squawking from the carrion.

And the outrider, and the broken bodies of the driver and guard, and the others scattered by the ambushers' bullets as they came crawling out of the wrecked, overturned coach.

And Lucy, still inside the coach, killed not by design but by accident, by a wild bullet that had sought her out and killed her just as surely as if it had been meant for her. He felt tears burning in his eyes, and that overpowering anger coming over him again. The gold? He would recover that if he could because recovering it was his job. But avenging Lucy—that was what he had really come here for. That he would do if he did nothing else.

He slept at last, an uneasy sleep in which he cried out involuntarily once or twice. He wakened a little before dawn, as he always did, and got to his feet instantly, wary and alert, listening to each early morning sound, the first chirping of the birds, the faint stirring of the early morning breeze.

While it was still dark, he kindled a small fire and heated water for coffee. He cooked a few strips of bacon and fried some cold biscuits in the bacon grease. He ate quickly, gulped the coffee, then cleaned up his utensils and put them away with his blanket roll.

He killed his fire and scattered it, then saddled up his horse. He mounted, and in the first gray light of dawn rode out along the trail made by the galloping men as they pursued him here last night. He followed the trail easily, for it consisted of deeply indented tracks made by horses ridden hard. Sooner or later, he knew, the men

31

would have stopped, discussed their failure to catch him and dispersed. Each would have gone separately to his home. Each would have left a separate, easily followed trail.

The sky continued to grow lighter, and at last the sun turned the high clouds pink. Tom Condon looked at the sky approvingly. The weather would slay clear for a couple of days at least. Nothing would erase these trails that meant so much to him. There would be time for following all of them.

Two miles past the place he had camped last night, he found where they had stopped. Here tracks of horses and men mingled and overlaid. But from this place, separate trails led away. It was just a matter of picking one at random and following it out. No matter which trail he chose, he would be led to a participant in the stagecoach attack, in the cold-blooded murder of Lucy and the stagecoach guards.

He selected a trail and touched the bay's sides lightly with his spurs.

CHAPTER 5

THE TRAIL LED NORTH, BACK TOWARD THE SERIES OF hills and ridges that mounted to the high peaks of the Divide. The air was chill, and a fog lay over some of the lower sections of the park, fog that slowly began to dissipate before the warm rays of the morning sun. Now and then Condon glanced behind, aware that he was visible in this rising land, aware also that he was a hunted man and would be so until he had either succeeded or failed at what he had set out to do. They'd shoot him on sight, these rebels, because they knew doing so gave them their only chance to survive and remain anonymous.

Thinking of Lucy and of the way she had looked lying dead within the overturned coach, he was glad the rebels would shoot on sight. It would justify his shooting back at them. It would eliminate any need to capture them alive.

He was ashamed of that thought almost immediately. He wasn't a killer—an executioner. But he couldn't be sure how he would react when he faced one of the men he knew to have been involved. He was aware that he might lose control of himself. He'd hunted down lawbreakers before but never for a wholesale slaughter such as this, never for a woman's wanton murder. Nor had he ever been involved personally before. Never before had he wanted to kill as badly as he did right now.

The trail was easily followed. The man he was tracking had employed no subterfuge. It had not, apparently, occurred to him or to the others that the hunted would turn hunter today, or that he would follow out the trails one by one.

Condon had not traveled more than half a dozen miles before he realized who he was tracking. Hal McCurdy had made this trail. Hal McCurdy's place was the only one within half a dozen miles of here.

He knew McCurdy slightly. He knew the man was unpredictable. He also knew McCurdy was dangerous, and wild, perhaps even unstable if he was drinking very much. And he probably had been drinking since that stagecoach attack. All the men were probably drinking, trying to forget. If they had consciences they were.

33

The sun climbed steadily across the morning sky. Condon entered a narrow canyon in the bottom of which a small stream ran. There was a rutted, two-track road here, going back and forth across the stream half a dozen times or more in every mile. The trail he was following stayed in the road but Condon wasn't watching the trail anymore. He was watching the land ahead, and his hand was never far from the grips of his holstered gun.

He stopped once and realized he was sweating in spite of the coolness of the air. He stared up at the canyon slopes, knowing if he had any sense he'd climb one of them and come on McCurdy's cabin from behind. Yet he was also aware of how short his allotted time already was. He had found one of the men he sought, but he still had to find the other six or eight. A good part of one day was gone.

Short of the last canyon bend, he stopped again. Now he swung his horse and tied the animal to a tree in the shelter of a sheer face of rock. He slid his rifle from the saddle scabbard and levered a cartridge into it slowly so that the gun's action would make no unnecessary noise.

He went on afoot, pausing momentarily when the cabin came into sight. His eyes narrowed as he watched it, as he searched the area around it for signs of life.

A thin plume of smoke rose from the rock chimney of the place. The front door was ajar.

It was a cabin built of logs, hand-hewn and notched so that the corners fit snugly together. It was chinked with straw and mud. The roof was of sod, over brush and stout spruce poles, the ends of which extended out from the walls at front and rear, forming a kind of overhang that protected the entryway.

Condon forced an unwilling patience into his

34

thoughts. He told himself that if McCurdy shot him here, the others would go unpunished. Worse, there could be a full-scale war down in the park in which dozens of innocent people would be killed.

He tried to remember how much family McCurdy had. A wife. He was sure of that. He also seemed to remember a half-grown boy.

Behind the cabin there was a little shed. From its door a man came suddenly, carrying an armload of wood. It was McCurdy and he threw one quick glance down-country toward the place where the road emerged from the narrowing canyon. He looked straight at Condon, but he apparently did not see him, for he looked away, went into the cabin, and slammed the door behind him. After a moment the smoke coming from the stone chimney thickened as he added more firewood to the stove.

Condon moved cautiously. He approached the cabin, staying in the creek bottom where he was mostly concealed by willows and by brush. He was halfway to the cabin before he had decided what he was going to do. The best way was the most direct. He'd get to the cabin door without alerting McCurdy and his family if he could. He'd fling open the door and plunge inside before any of the three even knew that he was here. It was his best chance of avoiding bloodshed. It was his only change of taking McCurdy alive.

Abreast of the cabin, he left the shelter of the creek bottom. Running, he crossed the small clearing and halted on the blind side of the cabin where there were neither windows nor doors.

He was out of breath. His lungs labored, as much from excitement as from the short run getting here.

All was still quiet inside the house. He wondered

briefly if McCurdy was waiting for him inside, gun leveled at the door, ready to shoot the instant he came plunging in.

It was a possibility. The house was quiet, perhaps quieter than it ought to be. He clenched his jaws, hesitated a moment, then carefully leaned the rifle against the cabin wall. Drawing his revolver, he eased the hammer back, then moved cautiously toward the corner of the house.

He wished he could quiet his breathing more, but a strange urgency was pushing him, an urgency that would not let him wait. His mind was seeing Lucy's dead face, so pale there within the coach. His thoughts were remembering how twisted and stiff she had been, stiffened in a position that did not even permit his taking her back to Unionville with him. Instead he'd had to go in without her, sending others back with the hearse to do what he should have done himself.

He would not even be there for her funeral. He'd be here instead, or down in the park on Grizzly Creek, or in the little settlement they called Davistown after the president of the Confederacy. He'd be avenging her, and he could start right now, inside this cabin, no more than a dozen feet away, was a man who could have fired the bullet that took her life.

He reached the corner of the cabin. He saw that he would have to pass a window before he could reach the door. He got down on his hands and knees and slowly crawled under it, getting up only when he was past.

Now the door was ahead. It had a latch type fastener operated by a leather thong that hung outside.

He took hold of the latchstring with one hand, holding the cocked revolver in the other. His mouth was a thin, hard line, his eyes narrowed and very cold.

Suddenly he yanked the latchstring and flung wide the door.

He did not stand in the doorway but leaped instantly inside. He ducked to one side of the door, putting his back to the roughhewn wall. He roared, "Hold it, McCurdy. Hold it or I'll blow your head off!"

The cabin had only one room and a loft. It had windows on this side, through which streamed the morning sunlight. It was also lighted by the open door. There was a table in the center of the room, and there was a stove beyond. There were a couple of other chairs and there was a bed.

A woman stood beside the stove, turned to face him, her hands clasped together nervously. Her hair was untidy and her eyes were terrified. His gun covered her briefly, then passed on, its deadly muzzle searching.

McCurdy stood beside the table, and it was plain that he had been surprised. He stared at Condon unbelievingly. His eyes flashed toward the corner where a double-barreled shotgun leaned, then back toward the loft, the floor of which creaked suddenly with some movement there.

Condon's gun swung past McCurdy toward the loft, in time to see a rifle poke its gaping, large-bore snout toward him. He had the swiftest glimpse of a scared young face behind the gun and bawled, "Kid, put it away! I don't want—"

The rifle roared, smoke billowing from its muzzle, striking the wall and spreading until it all but filled the room. The bullet tore into the log wall a foot from Condon's head.

But the threat was gone. That had been a muzzle loader and it was doubtful if the boy had another weapon in the loft. Besides that, the recoil had knocked

37

the boy flat. Neither gun muzzle nor scared young face was visible anymore.

McCurdy had used the interruption to lunge across the room and seize the double-barreled shotgun leaning against the wall. He was turning now, his mouth twisted, his eyes completely wild. He was turning and the gun was coming up.

There would be no escape from the shotgun. Not at close quarters. There *could* be no escape.

Condon shouted, "No! I don't want. . . " And then he knew he was out of time. He had already delayed too long. McCurdy hadn't had to seize that shotgun, but he had, and now there was nothing Condon could do but defend himself.

He fired instantly and did not wait to see what effect his bullet might have had. The twin bores of the shotgun filled his mind. He had seen the damage a charge of shot could do at close range. The thing would cut him clean in two. He flung himself aside, letting himself fall helplessly.

The awful roar of the shotgun filled the room, deafening, sending shooting pains through Condon's head from both tortured eardrums. It felt as though a dozen bees had stung his arm and shoulder, and then his body hit the floor and he knew he was still alive. He'd been stung, but he wasn't dead.

He rolled, not knowing whether he'd hit McCurdy or not. He stopped and raised his gun for another shot.

McCurdy sat down at that instant, sat down on the floor, the smoking shotgun still clutched in both his hands. There was an expression of surprise on his face. The wildness had gone from his unstable eyes.

Condon pushed against the floor with his hands and came up to his knees. Watching McCurdy, he got cautiously to his feet. Out of the corner of his eye, he kept tabs on the woman, who had not moved from the stove. Behind him, he could hear the ragged breathing of the boy up in the loft.

Suddenly he saw a red stain appear on the front of McCurdy's shirt, left side center. It spread as he watched until it was as big as one of his hands. McCurdy must have felt the warmth of blood because he looked down at the stain, then up again at Condon. "You son-of-a-bitch!" he said.

Condon didn't reply. There was nothing to argue about. McCurdy knew what he had done. He knew Condon knew or he wouldn't have gone for the shotgun so recklessly. He had gambled and lost and now he was paying up.

There was a flurry of movement in the loft behind Condon, but before he could turn his head to look, he was struck hard from above and behind by the boy, who had leaped from the loft upon his back.

The impact drove him forward and down onto the floor. His body cushioned the boy's fall, but the air was driven from his lungs and he was suddenly as helpless as a fish on a river bank. But he wasn't helpless enough to release his gun when the boy tried to pry it out of his hand. Instead, he cuffed the boy roughly, his face gray and sweating. He was fighting for breath with little, frantic gasps.

There was surprising strength and power in his swinging arm and open hand and the boy was flung away from him, across the room and against the table leg. Condon got a brief glimpse of the youngster's face. It was filled with terror more terrible than any he had ever seen. The boy's eyes were wide, his face pale and drawn, his lips compressed and almost blue. There was sudden shock in him that he could frighten the boy this much, and then he heard the woman moving on the other side of the room.

Helplessly he turned his head to look at her. She was crossing the room toward her husband now, an expression of resolution on her face. She reached McCurdy, knelt before him, and looked at him. It was plain she knew her husband had only a few minutes to live at most.

The shotgun lay across McCurdy's legs. She lifted it, got to her feet, and turned. She raised the gun and stared at Condon over the twin bores.

The boy began to sob brokenly. That and Condon's terrible fight for breath were the only sounds in the smoke-filled room.

It seemed an eternity that she stood there, the shotgun leveled at him, the hammer back, her finger curled over the trigger. But suddenly there were other sounds, those of the boy scrambling to his feet, plunging across the room.

His voice came out shrill and high, almost like a scream. "Ma! No! Don't do it, Ma!"

Condon knew he had never been closer to death in his life before. In a second, in part of a second, that gun would fire and he would be dead.

But it was too late now to move, too late for doing anything. With eyes that seemed hypnotized, he stared at the wavering muzzle of the gun.

The boy, moving fast, plunged between him and the woman with the gun and at that instant the gun discharged. Again it seemed as though bees were stinging him, but again he was still alive because he had not caught the full force of the charge.

The room filled again with smoke. It made his eyes

burn and fill with tears. It made him choke and cough, and perhaps that started the air going in and out of his lungs once more.

With pain constant and terrible in his chest, he struggled to his feet. He stared in horror at the carnage in the room.

Mrs. McCurdy still stood where she had before, the smoking shotgun in her hands. Between her and the sheriff lay the boy, his chest a mass of torn and bloody flesh. McCurdy himself had fallen over, dead, his eyes still open but fixed on nothing now.

Head hanging, Condon stood, fighting hard for breath. The woman fainted, eyes closed, her face as gray as death.

He remained still for a moment more, then went to her, picked her up and carried her to the bed in the corner of the room. He laid her down, then pulled a blanket from the foot of the bed and went back to the boy. He wrapped the boy's bloody body in it and carried him outside. He returned for McCurdy, taking him beneath the shoulders and dragging him outside to lie beside his son. It would be better if Mrs. McCurdy didn't have to look at them when she regained consciousness.

He hadn't meant for it to end this way. He was sick, physically sick at the way things had turned out. He felt like vomiting.

He stood, spread-legged, over the two blanket-covered bodies in the bare yard and stared at nothing, his eyes numb and empty and cold. He muttered softly beneath his breath. "God damn the lousy, stinking, dirty war! God damn it all to hell!"

CHAPTER 6

CONDON WAS EXHAUSTED. HE SAT DOWN ON THE stoop and stared numbly at the two bodies in the yard. The sun was bright and warm. Looking out at the greening landscape, smelling the awakening earth, it seemed impossible to him that this had happened, that it could happen here, so far from the war raging between the states.

But it had happened, and McCurdy was dead, along with his son who had had nothing to do with the attack on the stagecoach but who had showed the courage to pitch in and help his father when the chips were down and he needed help.

Condon became aware of the wounds he had received from the shot. They had begun to burn and he peeled up his sleeve to look at them. In most cases, the shot was embedded less than a quarter inch, having made small holes that were now brown with drying blood. Somebody would have to pick the damn things out, one by one. But it would have to wait. There wasn't any time just now. At least the gun had been loaded lightly, for rabbits or for birds. If it had been loaded with buckshot he wouldn't have gotten off so easily.

His breathing was almost normal now. He walked across the yard and got a shovel from the shed. He went up behind the house to a place where there was already a small, white-painted wooden cross. He marked out two graves beside the older one and began to dig. He was conscious that this was costing time, time he needed desperately, but he also knew there was nothing else that he could do. He couldn't leave Mrs. McCurdy

42

alone with two dead bodies here. He owed it to her to give her this small amount of help.

He worked steadily and without haste, knowing from past experience exactly how much energy he could expend without having trouble with his breathing. The first grave began to deepen as he worked.

It took him completely by surprise, the shot from inside the house. He straightened, head turned, listening. His eyes widened. . .

He suddenly knew what he was going to find when he went back inside the house. He knew what he would find and he was sick with the certainty. He climbed wearily out of the grave he had been digging and hurried toward the house.

He reached the door and paused for a moment before going in. Then he stepped into the house, halting just inside the door.

She lay across the bed, her chest as torn and bloody as her son's chest had been. The shotgun, the trigger of which she must have pulled with a bare toe, lay on the floor beside the bed. A few little wisps of smoke rose from the shredded dress around the wound.

Tom Condon turned and plunged outside. The sun beat down hot upon him but in spite of it he was colder than he had ever been, ever before in his life. He began to shiver violently. His teeth chattered helplessly and even when he clenched his jaws with all his strength, they did not stop.

This family was dead, this whole family. Because of something McCurdy had done in the name of patriotism. Seven men and a woman killed on the Unionville stagecoach. Three more killed here. Nor was this the end. This couldn't be the end. There still were others as guilty as McCurdy had been.

43

Furiously, Condon stamped back up the hill. Furiously he marked out another grave. Furiously he began to dig again, working as though possessed. His breath grew short and still he worked. He sweated and fought for air, but still he worked. He worked until his hands were raw with broken blisters, until he was closer to exhaustion than he had been in a long, long time. He did not stop until he had finished the three shallow graves.

When he had finished, he stumbled down the hill, knees trembling with weariness. He picked up the body of the boy and carried it up the hill. He knelt beside the first grave and rolled it in. He climbed in after it and rearranged the blanket so that the body was covered. Then he staggered back for McCurdy.

He was forced to drag McCurdy up the hill as he had dragged him out of the house. The man was too heavy for him to lift.

Twice he stopped to rest, twice went on until at last he had rolled McCurdy into the second grave. He sat down and rested again.

The sun was in the western sky now, and starting to go down. A whole day gone. A whole day, and only one of the culprits caught. He didn't even know if McCurdy had hidden any of the gold here at his house. He might have cached it anywhere.

Reluctantly, dreading what he now must do, Condon got up and went slowly to the house. He went in, growing cold again. He crossed the room to the bed. He tried to avoid looking at Mrs. McCurdy's face, but found it was impossible. As he stared down at her he thought angrily, "He committed a crime. He was guilty of murder and it was my job to bring him in. I tried to do it without hurting anyone but he wouldn't let it be

44

that way." He realized he was trying to justify himself. But how could there be any justification for this, for a woman dead, and a boy dead, and a man dead for a single, unlawful act of the man?

He rolled her body up in a blanket, lifted it and carried it outside. He carried it up the hill without stopping to rest, and rolled it into the third grave. He was shaking with exhaustion when he had finished and his breath came in short, labored gasps. His chest felt as though a fire burned in it.

He was sick with regret, but there was something else growing in him now that had not been there before. It was anger, different from the anger he had felt since his discovery of the wrecked and looted stage, since his discovery of Lucy's body and those of the murdered guards. This was not a wild, flaring kind of anger that must eventually burn itself out. This was slower, like a bed of smoldering coals. It would burn on and on because it was the anger of helpless sorrow, not only for Lucy and the guards but for these three dead as well. For these three and for the others who would die before his job was done.

He had to have something to sustain him or he could not continue. Something deep within him knew this and kindled the anger to help him go on.

Slowly his breathing became normal again. His legs stopped trembling. Rising, he picked up the shovel and began to fill the graves.

He worked steadily for almost an hour. The sun slid down the sky toward the distant range of mountains in the west. At last he finished and walked back down into the yard. He leaned the shovel against the house.

Some freak effect of the breeze, or of the echoing canyon walls, carried the faintest of shouts to him. He

45

recovered his rifle leaning against the house, and running, hurried to the place he had left his horse. He untied him, mounted, and rode upstream hurriedly, hearing now the talk of the approaching men.

He had hoped all this might go undiscovered, at least for a while, but his hope was going to be denied. Riding as swiftly as he dared, he continued straight upstream, staying in the water to hide his tracks. He was glad the day was almost done. When those men saw what had happened at McCurdy's place, when they saw the blood inside the house and the three graves up on the hill. . . When they saw the tracks of Tom Condon's horse. . .

They'd hunt him with the same fanatical fury with which he was hunting them. They'd hunt him until he was dead or until they were. There could be no stopping now, for either side.

War had come to this vast and empty park. The first battles had been fought, the first dead put to rest. He could imagine what they were thinking, what they were saying now back there at McCurdy's house. They were accusing him, with furious revulsion and disgust, of being a mad-dog killer who had murdered not only McCurdy but his wife and boy as well. He'd never get a chance to tell his side of what had happened before they came. He was being tried and convicted back there right now. All that would remain afterward was to execute him. And the first man who saw him would do that. Or try.

Crawford, Hamidy, and Hobo Jennings pulled their horses to a halt immediately in front of the McCurdy cabin. The door stood ajar and Crawford shouted, "McCurdy!"

There was no reply. There was no sound. Crawford

46

looked puzzledly at Hamidy. "He ought to be here. Or if he ain't, his wife and kid ought to be here."

Hamidy looked disinterestedly at the door. He swung off his horse. "I'll take a look inside."

He went into the house. His voice came back. "Nobody's here, Crawford. The damn place is empty—" His voice stopped suddenly, and an instant later he yelled, "Hey! There's blood all over in here! It's on the floor an' on the bed."

Crawford dismounted hastily. He was not wearing his uniform today and looked considerably less imposing in ordinary clothes. He strode to the door, his bearing military if his dress was not. He went inside. Hobo Jennings also dismounted and followed him in. Crawford breathed, "Jesus!" He sniffed the air. "You can still smell the gunpowder." He crossed to the bed and picked up the shotgun. He sniffed the muzzle, then turned his head and stared at the other two. He looked at the spot of blood on the floor where McCurdy's son had lain, then back at the bloodstain on the bed. He said, "Where the hell are they? It looks like at least two people have been killed here today, but where are their bodies? Take a look outside."

Hamidy and Jennings went out the door. Jennings went on foot to the small shed. Hamidy mounted and began a circle of the area, carefully watching the ground for tracks. He picked up Condon's boot tracks arriving, and picking up the trail he had made as he left, plainly running now. Continuing, he found the three fresh graves on the hill behind the house, with Condon's boot tracks in plentiful supply around the graves. He shouted for Crawford.

Crawford came walking up the hill, with Jennings following. Hamidy pointed to the graves. "The son-of-a-

47

bitch murdered all three of 'em. He must have left when he heard us coming because I picked up his tracks, running, down there in front of the house."

Jennings asked, "Who?"

"Condon. Who else?"

"Maybe somebody else. Maybe somebody that was after the gold McCurdy had."

Hamidy said, "I told you we ought to have made everybody bring that gold to the settlement. Now we don't know where it is."

"There aren't many places he could have hidden it. Hobo, take the shed out there. Hamidy and I will take the house. Look in everything. Look for fresh-dug places in the floor."

Jennings stared at him doubtfully for a moment. Then he went down off the rise and entered the little shed. Crawford glanced at Hamidy. "You knew McCurdy. Where do you think he would have hidden it?"

"Not in the shed. He'd want it in the house with him."

"That's what I figured. But where in the house?"

Hamidy shrugged. "Let's go look. Maybe the mattress. Maybe the flour bin."

Crawford walked toward the house. He stopped just outside the door to glance toward the creek where Condon's trail had disappeared. Hamidy came up behind him and Crawford said, "We need that gold. We've got to find it before somebody else does. But I hate to let that damned killer get away. I hate to see him get away with this."

Hamidy's eyes brightened. His voice was tight as he said, "I could trail him."

Crawford turned his head and stared steadily at Hamidy. He felt a strange uneasiness. He felt as he sometimes had coming upon a rattlesnake—filled with a

48

combination of revulsion and fear. But he nodded reluctantly. "All right, go after him. But I want him brought in alive, do you understand?"

Hamidy nodded shortly, noncommittally. He turned and went to his horse. He mounted and rode away, heading for the creek.

CHAPTER 7

CONDON KNEW HE WOULD BE PURSUED. HE KNEW they would realize he had gone upstream, hiding his tracks in the water. And since riding in the water was slow and tedious, he climbed his horse out, selected a long draw leading away to the left, and put the horse into it.

He climbed steadily for half an hour, occasionally glancing behind toward the valley below. He saw Hamidy before the man saw him and reined immediately into a thick stand of pine.

He didn't like the way he was feeling this afternoon. His anger smoldered because he felt he had been unfairly put into a position he found impossible. He felt guilty, and there was no good reason why he should. He hadn't killed McCurdy's son. And McCurdy's wife had killed herself, overcome with remorse because she had accidentally killed the boy.

The truth of the matter was, he had done only what he should, what he was supposed to do. He had pursued McCurdy here and had acted in a way calculated to involve the least risk, for McCurdy. McCurdy's family, and himself. He could have done nothing else. Had he

49

called out a challenge, McCurdy would have fought. He'd have had to take the cabin by waiting until darkness fell and McCurdy would have been killed anyway.

But maybe not the way he had. Maybe his son wouldn't have become involved. And if the son had not butted in and been killed, Mrs. McCurdy wouldn't have felt compelled to kill herself.

Riding through the thick stand of timber, he cursed softly to himself. No amount of rationalizing was going to change anything. The McCurdy family was dead and he had buried them. Nothing he did or thought would bring them back. Neither would anything erase the guilt he felt. That burden he would have to carry, whether he wanted to or not.

But he could make himself stop thinking about the McCurdys. He could be thinking about the ones who had been on the stage, the ones so wantonly murdered by McCurdy and his friends. Lucy. Nate Widemeier, whose wife was grieving for him back in Unionville right now. Milt Snyder, who had left two half-grown children in Unionville when he volunteered to ride along and help guard the stage. And the others—the driver and the guard and the three who had been with Lucy inside the coach.

The real trouble was that guilt might make him act differently toward the others who were left. He might go soft, trying to avoid a repetition of what had happened at McCurdy's place. And softness just wouldn't do. Softness could bring on open warfare between the people of Unionville and the rebs at Grizzly Creek. Softness could result in the deaths of more innocent people. Softness could make him fail and he didn't dare to fail.

He wasn't worried about McCurdy's share of the stolen gold. The others would locate that. He doubted if any of them was interested in the gold for himself and knew that eventually it would all be gathered together in one place. It would be dispatched to the Confederacy in a single shipment and there was plenty of time to go after it when it was. Right now he was more interested in the men who had taken it.

Watching from the stand of pines, he saw Hamidy put his horse into the ravine and start climbing, his upturned face white in the fading light. There was no anxiety in Condon. He knew he would have no trouble staying ahead of Hamidy until dark. Instead, he was considering laying an ambush for the man. If he killed Hamidy now it would be one less to reckon with later on.

With this decided, he rode straight to the head of the ravine, forcing his horse to a trot on the thick carpet of damp pine needles covering the ground. The sound of hoofbeats was muffled, but when he reached bare ground at the head of the ravine, Condon slowed the animal to a walk.

Now he circled away from the trail he had made and started back watchfully. When he had returned a quarter of a mile back down the ravine, he tied his horse and continued on foot, first making sure that the wind was blowing crosswise to the ravine and would therefore neither carry the scent of his horse to Hamidy's nor that of Hamidy's horse to his.

Carefully, he worked his way toward the trail he had made earlier, conscious of how short the time had become. The sun was down, and the light it cast on the high and drifting clouds was fading too. Already it was growing dark beneath the pines. In another ten minutes the light would be too poor to shoot.

But there was another reason for hurrying. Hamidy must now be very close to the ambush point. If he had gone past it by the time Condon arrived. . .

But when he reached the place, he could hear Hamidy coming on from below, his horse making a racket in the rocky center of the ravine.

Condon cocked his rifle cautiously, muffling the metallic click of the hammer coming back with his other hand. His eyes narrowed as he stared downward through the fading light.

Hamidy rode into sight, his brow furrowed with concentration, his eyes fixed steadily on the trail.

He was a slight young man with a sallow skin. He had been in Unionville perhaps half a dozen times since his discharge from the Confederate Army so Condon knew who he was. He wore his gun low against his right side and, from the looks of the rig, Condon knew he would be good with it.

Condon always got a strange, vaguely uneasy feeling when he looked at Hamidy. It was the feeling he had had on the few occasions in his life when he had encountered a rattlesnake. It was revulsion, combined hatred and fear. It was something instinctive—like the fear humans have for snakes. There was something strange about Hamidy—something wrong.

As the man's horse climbed steadily toward him, Condon raised his rifle and put it against his shoulder. He lowered his head, resting his cheek against the cool wood of the rifle's stock. He closed an eye and sighted with the other one.

Hamidy reached the place where Condon's trail left the center of the ravine and entered the timber pocket at one side. He raised his head, halted his horse, and stared warily into the timber for a moment or two. He lifted his glance and observed the fading light in the sky. Then, decisively, he put his horse into the timber, urging him to a trot.

He was in range now. Condon slipped his finger through the trigger guard. He tightened it on the trigger, or tried to tighten it. He found that he could not.

He gritted his teeth angrily. Pulling a trigger was a simple thing, a thing he had done a thousand times before. He made himself think of Lucy, think of the way he had seen her last, but still he could not fire the gun. He could not be judge, jury, and executioner. Not after McCurdy and his wife and boy. Not after this afternoon.

Reluctantly, angry at himself, he lowered the rifle carefully.

Possibly, he thought, it is the cold-bloodedness of ambushing him that bothers me. He opened his mouth, preparatory to challenging Hamidy, then shut it suddenly. If he called out to Hamidy it would only give the killing an appearance of legality. He would know differently. Because even if he was warned, Hamidy wouldn't be able to protect himself. He'd be at too much of a disadvantage for that. It would be murder, just as much as shooting from ambush would. Or an execution by a self-appointed executioner taking upon himself the burden of responsibility he did not think the people of Unionville capable of carrying.

Selflessness could only go so far, he concluded sourly to himself. He had wanted to avoid bloodshed between the two communities if it was possible. Now he knew it wasn't possible.

Hamidy had gone, and with him daylight. Condon got to his feet and, walking silently on the carpet of needles underfoot, returned to his horse. He mounted and pointed the horse in the opposite direction, away from

53

Hamidy. He crossed over the first ridge, came out of the timber into the open country, and put his horse immediately into a lope, paralleling the slope.

He headed toward Unionville, frowning in the deepening dusk that crept like a shroud across the vast and open park. He closed his eyes and shook his head, wondering if he would ever forget that sight inside McCurdy's place.

He never would, he knew, anymore than he would forget Lucy and the way she had looked when he saw her last.

But he did know one thing certainly. He might be able to make peace with himself over McCurdy's death. He might even be able to absolve himself of the deaths of McCurdy's wife and son.

But not if he went on. Not if he found and executed the rest of those who had attacked the stage.

The people of Unionville would just have to shoulder their own burden, no matter what the cost.

CHAPTER 8

IN TOTAL DARKNESS, CONDON COVERED THE LAST miles into Unionville, his horse slogging all but blindly through the flooded meadows of the park. Ice crunched beneath his horse's hooves, a thin crust frozen by the night's early chill.

It was midnight when he arrived. He was cold and tired and gloomily irritable, hut hè knew he had to face the townspeople before he dared get any sleep. He intended to form a posse and he meant that the people of

Unionville should themselves pursue the men who had robbed the stage and killed the guards. But he was going to lead them. He wanted to be present to see that law and not mob rule prevailed.

The stagecoach was parked in the middle of the street in front of the Nugget Saloon, a graphic reminder of the attack. Even in the almost total darkness of the street he could see the dried mud plastered to its sides. He closed his eyes briefly, his face contorting as he remembered the way Lucy had looked lying in it dead. . .

He crossed to the tie rail in front of the Nugget and swung stiffly from his horse. He looped the reins around the rail.

There was light inside the saloon. The place was crowded, but no piano played. There were no boisterous shouts, just a steady hum of talk.

Condon went to the doors and stepped inside. Instantly the place was silent as all heads turned toward him, as all eyes rested on his face. He said, "I've been to Grizzly Creek. They were waiting for me this side of it so I don't suppose there's much doubt that they are the ones we want. I got away and next morning trailed one of them. It was Hal McCurdy and he put up a fight. He's dead and so are his wife and boy."

"What about the others? And what about the gold?"

They didn't seem to care that both McCurdy's wife and son were dead, he thought bitterly. They didn't even seem to care how they had died. He stared angrily at them a moment while the clamor grew. Other questions were yelled at him, questions he didn't bother answering. At last he raised a hand and waited until they had quieted. "I want a posse. We'll leave at dawn."

Now they all crowded forward, yelling, jostling. Condon pushed his way through them roughly, almost

55

savagely. He reached the bar and yelled at Jules LeClerc, who was tending bar, "Get a pencil and paper and write down their names."

Jules waddled heavily to the end of the bar. He rummaged beneath it a moment and came back with a stub of pencil and a sheet of paper torn from a ledger. Condon roared, "Quiet, damn it! Quit pushing. All of you who want to go can go, so take your time!"

That had the effect of quieting them somewhat. They began to talk among themselves while they waited for those ahead to give their names and move out of the way. As each man gave his name, LeClerc wrote it down laboriously, frowning with concentration as he did.

Condon suddenly felt as if he were all alone, even here in this noisy crowd. He said, "I'll be back in half an hour. Tell everybody to stay because I want to swear them in."

LeClerc nodded and Condon pushed his way to the door. He wanted to see Lucy's grave. He thought that perhaps if he did he could put out of his mind the three graves he had left on the hill behind McCurdy's place.

He untied his horse and led him down the street to the log livery barn. No one was there, so he unsaddled the horse himself, put him into a stall, and gave him a generous feeding of hay.

Leaving, he walked up the main street of the town and beyond to the cemetery on the top of a knoll they called Gold Hill. The only light was that cast upon the land by the stars, but it was enough to see the fresh graves and the white wooden crosses at their heads.

Kneeling before the first, he struck a match, cupping his hands to shield its flame from the cold night wind.

The name inscribed on the cross was Widemeier. He

56

went on to the next and the next one after that. Lucy's was the fifth.

He straightened and stared down at it somberly, trying to remember Lucy's face. He was shocked to realize it was fading from his memory. Already it was hazy, clouded, receding in his thoughts.

He frowned, trying desperately to make it clear. Instead it was replaced in his memory by the worn, aging face of McCurdy's wife, dead and white as he had seen it last. Then even that faded and all he could see were the three mounded graves and all he could feel was utter exhaustion of both body and spirit. The bodies here cried out to be avenged and he knew they had to be avenged. The people of Unionville wouldn't rest until they were, no matter what he did, no matter what he thought.

War was to blame for the attack on the stagecoach and the theft of the gold. However unbelievable it was, the war had come to this remote place in Colorado territory. Now it would spread and grow, as it had spread across the Southern states. It would go on until either one side or the other had been wiped out. Condon was a realist. He knew he couldn't stop what had to happen here. All he could do was try and give it a semblance of legality.

He turned from the grave and made his way down the hill to the head of Union Avenue. Somewhere he could hear a child crying fitfully.

He trudged down the street to the saloon and went inside. He crossed to the bar and picked up the paper Jules LeClerc pushed toward him. He shouted, "I'll read off your names. I want each of you to answer when I call your name. Afterward I'll administer the oath."

He called off the first name and a man answered,

"Here." He went on, pausing after each name until the man had answered him. Then he yelled, "Raise your right hands."

More than fifty hands went up. He said, "Do you swear to uphold the laws of the Territory of Colorado and of this county to the best of your ability?"

There was a shouted chorus of replies. "All right," Condon yelled, "we'll meet in front of this saloon at dawn. Each man is to furnish his own horse, gun, and rations for two days. Go home now and get some sleep."

He needed sleep himself. But he waited at the bar until the last of them had filed noisily out through the swinging doors into the night. The saloon was almost empty now. He turned to LeClerc and said, "Give me a bottle and a glass."

Jules slid him a bottle and followed it with a glass. Condon poured himself half a glass of whiskey and gulped it down. It made a warm glow in his throat and stomach. He poured a second one and drank it. A voice asked, "What are you going to do, ride over there and burn Davistown the way Quantrill burned Lawrence, Kansas?"

Condon turned his head. The speaker was Lucy's father—Thomas Wiley, a slight man, balding, with deep-set eyes.

"I wouldn't have thought *you'd* care," Condon said.

"Lucy was killed by a handful of criminals during the commission of a crime," Wiley said. "I want them brought to justice—hanged if that is the decision of the court. I don't want vengeance against the whole community of Davistown."

Condon stared at him. He was tired, and his irritability was close to the surface. Wiley was a thinker, not a doer. He got out a camp newspaper once a week

58

and he deplored violence. "You make it sound so easy," Condon said. "But how do you separate the crime they committed from their reason for committing it? They wanted that gold for the Confederacy. That makes it part of the war whether you like it or not."

Wiley stubbornly shook his head.

Condon frowned with exasperation. "All right then. How would you handle it? The people of Davistown will protect the identity of the men who attacked the stage. If I take a posse over there they'll probably fight. The only answer is to take a large enough posse either to discourage them or to win, no matter what."

"I thought you were going to handle it yourself."

"I intended to." Condon lifted his glance to Wiley's. "I trailed McCurdy home from the place they tried to ambush me. I figured the only way I could take him alive was to bust in on him. Only it didn't work out that way. I got McCurdy when he tried to kill me. His wife took up the fight and accidentally killed the boy when he tried to stop her from killing me. While I was burying McCurdy and the boy, she shot herself."

"And you blame yourself?"

"You're damned right I do. Wouldn't you? If I'd taken a posse over there, it's doubtful if McCurdy would have put up a fight. Even if he had, it wouldn't have involved his wife and son."

"You can't know that."

"Maybe not. But I do know one thing. I shouldn't have to do it all by myself. It's the responsibility of every one of the people here. Besides, I think that if the posse I take to Davistown is big enough, they might just give up. Maybe there won't have to be a fight."

"You could call on the military for help. There's a garrison in Denver and that's only ninety miles away."

Condon shook his head. "It's too far and there isn't time. The gold would be gone before a troop of cavalry could get up here."

"Is the gold so important to you?"

"Hell yes, it is. If it gets away it's going to help the Confederacy. It could result in prolonging the war. It could cost the lives of a couple of hundred men."

"Or the deaths of a hundred here. Did you happen to notice that both Holley and Duckworth are going along with you?"

"I noticed."

"Do you think they're going to let you stay in control?"

Condon studied him patiently. "What would you suggest I do? Forget the whole damn thing?"

"You could get the cavalry here from Denver. You could let them take over."

"They wouldn't do it, Wiley. They have no jurisdiction. We know where that gold is going, but we have no proof. This is a civil matter to be handled by the sheriff's office."

"The cavalry would intervene if local authorities certified that the law had broken down and asked for help."

"But it hasn't broken down." The patience was fading from Condon's voice. Wiley had opposed Lucy's marriage to him from the first, not because he disliked him or because there was anything wrong with his character but because of the profession he was in. Wiley's philosophy was that the meek would inherit the earth. Condon's wry comment had been, "Maybe, but not this part of it."

"It will break down. You won't be a dozen miles from here before Holley and Duckworth will be in control of your posse. Before you get to Davistown, they'll have turned it into a mob."

"I guess you'll have to let me worry about that." Condon pushed a coin across the bar to pay for his drinks. He turned, crossed the room, and went out the door into the night.

His quarters adjoined the jail. His tiny room, which opened off the square log building, contained a bed, a stove, a dresser, and a washstand. Condon only slept in here; he spent most of his time in the sheriff's office, which occupied the front half of the jail building.

He sat down on the edge of the bed and pulled off his boots.

He was thinking about Holley and Duckworth as he removed his pants and shirt, blew out the lamp, and got in bed.

Holley had been a captain in the war. He had lost an eye to a saber thrust and had been discharged. Duckworth had been a sergeant under him. Condon didn't know why Duckworth had been discharged. The two were inseparable though the relationship was not that of two equals. Holley was still "captain" to Duckworth. Duckworth was still "sergeant" to Holley.

Both of them were fond of reminiscing about the war, telling stories of their exploits. Condon realized that Wiley was right about one thing. Holley *would* try to take control of the posse as soon as it left town. Duckworth *would* support him. And if Holley succeeded in getting control of it, he'd turn it into a military force. He'd attack Davistown and slaughter its inhabitants. He'd burn it to the ground.

Condon closed his eyes. Perhaps he had been wrong in coming back. Perhaps he had been wrong in letting the deaths of Mrs. McCurdy and her son get to him the

61

way they had.

But he knew the people of Unionville wouldn't have waited more than another day in any case. He wouldn't have been able to do much in that length of time.

He slept at last, an uneasy sleep from which he wakened several times before he finally got up half an hour before dawn began to gray the sky.

CHAPTER 9

MAJOR JEFFERSON CRAWFORD WATCHED HAMIDY ride away. He was frowning faintly. Something about Hamidy bothered him, but he knew that if anyone could trail the man that had killed McCurdy and his family, Hamidy could.

Crawford wondered if the killer had found the gold. He turned worriedly and went into the house.

There was evidence of a struggle but none of a search having been made. Frowning, Crawford let his eyes roam around the room. There would be several logical places for hiding gold, places like the flour bin or sugar can. There would be other hiding places that were not so obvious. McCurdy hadn't been a fool. He wouldn't have hidden the gold in a place that was too obvious.

Crawford passed up the bed. He got down on his hands and knees and peered under the cast-iron cooking stove, but without finding anything. He went on, past a table that sat beneath a window in which a number of potted plants grew.

He stopped and reached for one of the potted plants. The soil was loose as if it had recently been disturbed.

Crawford dumped the pot onto the table and found a buckskin sack of gold dust in the bottom of the pot.

He dumped the others, but he only found two more sacks. He smiled. McCurdy *had* been smart. Even if someone had found the gold, they'd only have found half of it. And unless they had been on the raid themselves, they'd have had no way of knowing that each man had carried away six sacks.

He left the three sacks on the table and went on. He made a complete circle of the room, occasionally poking into some corner but without finding any more of the gold.

He turned his attention to the loft, climbing the ladder to it. There was a pile of rumpled bedding here where apparently McCurdy's son had slept. He stirred it with his foot.

Beneath it there was a little pile of dry earth. Crawford glanced up at the ceiling.

It was made of brush laid over poles. Over the brush was sod. Some of the dirt from the sod had sifted down through the brush. But why was it under the boy's bed instead of on top of it? Unless someone had moved the boy's bed while he stood here and. . .

Smiling faintly, he stuck his hand up to probe the brush between the poles. His hand encountered a buckskin sack.

He pulled it out and rummaged around until he found the other two. He tossed them down onto the bed, then climbed down the ladder, awkwardly because he only had one hand. He went to the door and yelled for Jennings.

It was now dusk and the sky was gray. Jennings brought the horses and loaded the gold sacks into the saddlebags of Crawford's horse. "Where'd you find 'em?"

"Three in the flowerpots, three in the ceiling above the loft. We were lucky this time, Next time we might not find it at all."

"What do you mean, next time?"

"I mean that Condon was the one who killed McCurdy and his family. Nobody else but Condon would have taken time to bury them. And Condon isn't going to quit."

"How the hell did he know . . . ?"

"That McCurdy was in on the raid? He followed McCurdy's tracks from where we waited to ambush him."

Jennings stared at Crawford worriedly. "He'll—"

"He won't do anything tonight. He's got Hamidy to worry about."

"Then let's get back to town."

Crawford nodded and swung onto the back of his horse. If Condon knew McCurdy had been involved in the stagecoach attack, he must know the others had also come from Grizzly Creek. Inevitably he would bring a posse to attack Davistown. Perhaps it would be tomorrow, perhaps the day afterward. But it wouldn't be very long.

Crawford supposed he would be wise to post some guards tonight around the edges of the town. He felt a stir of the old excitement at the prospect of doing battle once again. He wished he had a company of regulars instead of a handful of undisciplined gold-seekers, but he'd have to make do with what he had. Victories had been salvaged by outnumbered forces in the past. A victory could be salvaged out of this, if he planned carefully. First, though, he wanted to get the gold safely on its way. He didn't want to lose that if he should

64

happen to be defeated in the coming fight.

All the gray faded from the sky as they rode single file across the soggy flats. The stars winked out. He'd heard no shots so he had to assume Hamidy had failed to catch up with Condon before the sky grew dark.

He rode slouched in his saddle, his head sagging forward onto his chest, yet in spite of his relaxed position, there was something military about the silhouette he made. Hobo Jennings rode behind him, also slouched. The stump of Crawford's missing arm began to ache in the cold night air.

He was thinking about the war and about the way he had hated being forced out of it. The war had given him a reason for being, after Daisy died. But now, perhaps, he could feel alive again, and useful. In the end, if the people of Unionville were defeated and driven out of the park, their claims would be available to the Southerners of Davistown. Not only would the Confederacy have benefited. The people of Davistown would have benefited individually.

Crawford didn't give a damn about getting the gold himself. He wanted more than gold. He wanted the Confederacy to recognize what he had done. He smiled faintly to himself. Maybe President Davis would pin a medal on his chest. They might even find a place for him in the government.

The miles dragged, but eventually Crawford saw the lights of Davistown ahead. At the edge of town, he turned his head and looked at Jennings. "Ring the fire bell. I want everybody at the hotel in fifteen minutes."

Jennings scowled at him and started to say something, then changed his mind. Crawford watched him ride ahead. Jennings resented taking orders from him. Some of the others also did. But they took them because the

65

raid on the Unionville stagecoach had been his idea and because he brought it off successfully.

Jennings began to ring the fire bell. It brought people to their doors, brought them running into the street. Crawford heard Jennings yell, "The Major wants everybody in town at the hotel in fifteen minutes! Everybody!"

Crawford rode to the hotel and swung stiffly from his horse. The stump of his missing arm was aching horribly from the cold and the pain made him irritable.

Hamidy came riding up the street and dismounted beside Crawford. He said, "Find the gold?"

Crawford nodded. "Did you catch up with Condon?"

Hamidy shook his head. "It got too dark to trail."

"It doesn't matter. He'll come to us."

Crawford looped his horse's reins around the rail and stiffly went into the hotel. It was a huge barn of a place, built of logs and rough-sawed lumber. There was a stairway leading up to the rooms on the second floor. The lower floor was occupied by a lobby, a dining room, and a kitchen. The lobby was the biggest room in town, the only one capable of holding everybody. Crawford went to the bar and ordered a drink, which he gulped quickly. He poured another and gulped that too. The ache in his arm ought to be easing off soon. The whiskey would help. So would the heat radiating from the big pot-bellied stove in the middle of the room.

Hamidy and Jennings had followed him in. Now others began to come in from the street, stamping the mud off their boots just inside the door. One by one they crossed to the bar and ordered drinks. A few women were among them, some with children, most without.

Crawford waited. There were probably sixty or seventy people in Davistown, he thought. There were

66

maybe another twenty men scattered around in cabins within half a dozen miles of town. All told, he could probably muster forty or fifty men.

Of those who had helped attack the stage, Coyne, Jennings, Hamidy, Fall, Stebbins, and Goldsmith were here.

McCurdy and Stocker were dead. Hamidy, standing at Crawford's elbow, said, "That's about all of them."

Crawford raised a hand. They quieted. He shouted, "You all know about the attack on the Unionville stage. You know how successful it was. What you don't know is that the sheriff has apparently put two and two together and decided the men who attacked it came from here."

Someone yelled, "He can't prove it, can he?"

"He doesn't have to prove it. He'll be here with a posse either tomorrow or the day after. He'll search. He'll question. He'll end up with the gold and the men that robbed the stage, and the boys fighting for the Confederacy will go on being hungry and cold and they'll keep right on trying to win a war without bullets or cannonballs."

"What can we do?"

Crawford drew himself to his full height. The stump had stopped aching now. There was a warm glow in him from the whiskey he had drunk. He roared, "We can fight, that's what! We can do what the boys back home are doing, by God! If we win, we can go to Unionville and take over the best of the claims. Jeff Davis will go on getting the gold he needs and we'll be getting some for ourselves as well." He happened to glance at Hamidy. The man's expression was tense. There was a set smile on his face. Someone yelled, "What do you want us to do?"

"Go home and arm yourselves. Each of you saddle a horse and meet here two hours before dawn. I'm going to set up an ambush and let Condon walk into it! We'll wipe him and his outfit out."

There was some grumbling in the crowd. A man said sourly, "We ain't soldiers and this ain't the war. Condon's sheriff, and this is part of the county he's sheriff of."

The grumbling began to spread from the man who had spoken. Crawford jabbed a finger at him contemptuously. "Step up here, Jethro, and say that where everybody can hear. Then tell 'em the real reason you're doing so much grumbling. Tell them you're scared to fight."

Jethro's face flushed. He made no move to step forward, but he stopped grumbling and those around him also stopped.

Crawford glared at the men in the crowd. "You people here haven't got a choice. Not anymore. Condon knows we've got the gold. He's coming here to get it back and to take the men responsible. He's not going to care if a few of you get hurt while he's doing it. He's not going to care if he destroys this town."

A woman began to cry. Crawford repeated, "Go home and arm yourselves. It's the only way you're going to survive."

He watched them as they filed from the hotel. A few were hurrying eagerly, but these were mostly the younger ones. The ones old enough to have families were sober and subdued. But they all knew he had been right. They didn't have a choice. Men had been killed on the Unionville stage. Lucy Wiley had been killed and Lucy had been engaged to marry the sheriff. Condon would want more than just to recover the stolen gold.

68

He'd want revenge for Lucy's death.

Crawford glanced at Hamidy. Coyne and Jennings stood beyond him at the bar. Fall and Goldsmith were also waiting as though expecting special instructions from Crawford with respect to the gold.

He said, "Go home and get the gold and bring it back here. We can get it across the pass before daylight if we start right away."

The men nodded and hurried out the door into the night. Crawford followed and headed for the livery barn. It would take three pack animals to haul the gold. There ought to be another for bedding and supplies. Plus two saddle animals for the men who were to accompany the gold. He figured Fall and Goldsmith were the men for that. They seemed to have steadier nerves than anyone else in town.

CHAPTER 10

TWO OF THE DAVISTOWN GOLD-SEEKERS HUNG BACK after leaving the door of the hotel. They moved uncertainly into the darkness beside it and waited there. Joe Danvers was one of these, a big, bearded, dirty man of fifty. Kiley Lootens was the other, small and quick, with a diffident, apologetic manner. When the street was deserted, Danvers rumbled softly, "Crawford and Hamidy and the other five are still inside."

"What do you think they're up to, Joe?"

"I've been wondering. Suppose you was Crawford and suppose you figured Condon was coming here with a posse at dawn. What would you be doing between

69

now and then?"

"Getting rid of the gold?"

Joe Danvers nodded. "That's what I figure he'll have to do. He'll get it loaded and on its way so that no matter who wins the fight tomorrow, the South will get the gold."

"How do you reckon they'll take it out?"

"Over the pass to Denver on pack mules."

"What do we do, go up there and wait for them?"

Danvers shook his head. "Too risky. They'll be on guard and there will probably be five or six of 'em."

"What, then?"

Danvers was silent a moment Then he said, "We watched 'em when they came back from the raid. They didn't have any pack mules, which meant the gold had to have been split up evenly between them. They haven't been guarding any particular place in town since then which means each man still has part of the gold hidden out in his house."

"And now they're going to go after it and bring it all back , here?"

"Right. Let's take Hobo Jennings first. He's the one I like the least."

Kiley nodded and the two moved away into the darkness. Swiftly they went down the muddy, rutted street.

Davistown wasn't much different from Unionville. It was composed mostly of log buildings, but there were a few made of rough-sawed pine. There was also a liberal sprinkling of tents. Down at the lower end of town Grizzly Creek flowed south at right angles to the town's main street. Along both banks were sluice boxes and the excavations made by the gold-seekers. Here and there a claim notice nailed to a tree or stake fluttered white in the chill night wind. The claims were poor and gave up little gold. The miners made only enough to keep them digging and sluicing and panning but not enough to pay them more than scant wages for their time.

Hobo Jennings' house was a one-room shack made of slabs. Strips of canvas, hide, and cloth had been nailed over the cracks to keep out the wind. Danvers stopped in front of the shack, listening, until Lootens whispered nervously, "Let's get out of sight, for Christ's sake. He might he coming along at any time."

The creek made a steady roaring as it tumbled over the rocks a dozen yards away. The wind sighed through a tall pine beside the house. A light plume of smoke came from the chimney and drifted away on the wind. Kiley Lootens discovered that he was shivering and hoped Danvers hadn't noticed it. He was scared but not scared enough to run away. He kept thinking of those fat buckskin sacks of gold.

Danvers whispered hoarsely, "All right, let's get out of sight."

The two melted into the shadows beside the house. They waited for what seemed an eternity before they heard the sound of footsteps coming down the street from the direction of the hotel. Danvers whispered, "It's him. Quiet, now. Don't move."

Hobo Jennings had a horse. He was leading it. He tied it to a scrub tree in front of the house and, whistling almost soundlessly, opened the door and went inside. After a moment of audible fumbling around, a match flared, A moment later a lamp flickered, throwing light on the ground outside the door.

Danvers carefully pulled a strip of cloth away from one of the cracks between the slabs. It made an opening

71

a quarter of an inch wide, no more. But he could see inside the room. He could see Hobo Jennings' midsection and his hands, even if he couldn't see his face.

Jennings poured himself half a cup of coffee. He dumped whiskey from a brown bottle in on top of it. He sat down at the table and stared at the lamp, his face visible now that he was sitting down.

Kiley whispered, "What's he doing?"

"Shut up." The noise of the wind and of the creek drowned their whispers, but Danvers gripped Lootens' arm anyway to keep him still. Jennings continued to sip the coffee and whiskey mixture. At last he put the cup down and got to his feet. He went straight to the woodbox and turned it over on its side. Boards had been nailed across the bottom of it on two sides, forming supports that kept it off the floor, and also forming a space in which a small compartment had been built to hold the sacks of gold. Jennings withdrew them, one by one, and laid them on the table in a row.

Danvers whistled soundlessly. "He's got six of 'em," he whispered. "At fifteen pounds apiece, that's ninety pounds of gold. We're lookin' at more'n twenty-five thousand dollars worth."

Lootens pushed his face up close. "Lemme see."

"Time enough for that later. Cover me."

He moved away from the crack between the slabs, toward the open door of the shack. His gun was in his hand, but he hadn't thumbed the hammer back. He didn't want a gunshot giving them away, bringing everyone in camp there at a run.

He couldn't tell what Jennings was doing now, but the door was stilt ajar; the lamp cast a pale shaft of light out through it. Danvers halted short of the light and waited, his breath coming in short, uneven gasps. If Jennings didn't come out soon . . .

The lamp went out. Danvers crouched, gun fisted in his hand. He took a step closer to the door.

Suddenly Hobo Jennings was there, less than a yard away from him. He heard the faint scuff of Jennings' feet. He felt the man's movements, there so close to him. He raised the gun and struck blindly.

The gun connected with one of Jennings' shoulders and glanced off. Danvers moved in, frantic suddenly, afraid Jennings would make an outcry.

Behind Danvers, Lootens barked, "Get him, Joe! Don't let him get away!"

Danvers was trying, but Hobo was attempting to get away. He was badly hampered by the sacks of gold he carried in his arms. Ninety pounds was a lot of weight and a man couldn't move fast carrying it.

Suddenly Jennings released the gold. It dropped soddenly into the mud at his feet. With his hands free, he snatched frantically for his gun.

Danvers brought his own gun slashing down, trying for Jennings' head. Instead it cracked Jennings' forearm and sent his gun spinning into the mud a dozen feet away.

Jennings yelled, "Help! Hey—"

Danvers closed with him. One of his great arms encircled Hobo's neck. His free hand clamped over Jennings' mouth, stifling any further outcry. Jennings tried to bite the hand, without success. It was clamped too tightly for that.

Between clenched teeth, Danvers said, "Look sharp, Kiley. Somebody might have heard him yell."

Lootens stepped away from the struggling pair, his eyes probing the darkness in the direction of the town.

73

Jennings was still struggling in Danvers' grasp, but his struggles were weakening. He hadn't been able to take a breath since Danvers seized him a couple of minutes earlier.

Jennings went limp in Danvers' arms. Danvers released him and let him slide down into the mud.

Instantly Jennings was scrambling away, his breath rasping in and out of his starving lungs. He had feigned unconsciousness and it had worked. Temporarily at least.

Danvers lunged at him, fisted gun crashing down. There was a brief struggle on the muddy ground. Danvers' gun rose and fell, rose and fell, rose and fell as he hammered Jennings' skull with murderous brutality. All the while he kept muttering, "You son-of-a-bitch! You dirty son-of-bitch! Trying to make me believe you was dead when all the time. . ."

Kiley Lootens pulled him off. "Quit it, Joe! Stop making all that noise! Somebody's going to hear!"

Danvers got up. He was breathing heavily. Kiley said, "Let's get the gold and get the hell out of here. Jennings is dead, ain't he?"

"If he ain't, he ought to be." Danvers knelt, fumbled, and found one of the sacks of gold. Kiley knelt beside him, groping too. When each had three sacks, they got up and shuffled hurriedly back up the main street of the town. Halfway to the hotel, Danvers cut through a vacant lot to a shack on a knoll behind the town. The pair went in and Danvers closed the door. He dumped the three heavy buckskin sacks on the rumpled bed, then found a match, lighted it, and touched it to the wick of the coal-oil lamp.

He sat down on the edge of the bed and untied the thong around the neck of one of the sacks. He poured nuggets and dust out into the palm of his hand. He began to smile and the smile grew steadily wider. He began to laugh. He noticed blood on his right hand and wiped the hand ineffectually on his muddy pants. He stopped laughing long enough to say, "We're rich, Kiley! By God, we're rich!"

Kiley seemed stunned. He sat on the end of the bed, three of the heavy sacks in his hands. He was staring at a spot on the wall across the room, but he wasn't seeing it. His stare was blank. His mouth was partly open and he breathed through it heavily.

They sat this way for a long, long time. At last a crafty look came into Danvers' eyes. "We'd better hide it, Kiley. We'd better hide it someplace where it can't be found. We don't dare leave camp until the fight with Condon's posse is over with. If we do they'll know."

"Unless somebody else gets blamed for this. Like Condon, maybe. He jumped McCurdy, didn't he? It shouldn't be hard to make people believe he jumped Hobo Jennings too."

"But we're not supposed to show up til dawn."

"We can be anxious, can't we? We can show up earlier."

Danvers chuckled softly. He got up suddenly, picking up three sacks. "Let's hide it. Let's put it under that big rock out back."

Kiley Lootens picked up his own three sacks and followed Danvers out. The stars gave off enough light to see the big rock on the slope behind the shack. Kiley lifted one side of it, while Danvers shoved the sacks underneath. Afterward he propped the big rock up with a smaller one. They could have hollowed out a place for the buckskin sacks, but the loose earth might have given away their hiding place. This way, nothing was noticeable. Nothing was out of place.

There was a small corral about fifty yards from the shack. Inside were two horses and a mule. Each man caught a horse and saddled him. Leaving the horses at the door of the shack, the two went in, got rifles and ammunition and a gunnysack filled with food. Joe blew out the lamp and closed the door. They mounted and rode down the slope toward the hotel.

Already the men who had attacked the Unionville stage were gathering. Major Crawford was there and so was Coyne. Hamidy and Stebbins rode up and Fall and Goldsmith arrived a few minutes afterward.

"Where's Hobo?" Coyne asked. "I didn't see any light down there in his shack."

Crawford said, "You and Goldsmith go down and look. But come right back. We're getting short of time."

Coyne mounted and Goldsmith followed suit. The two rode down the muddy street toward Hobo Jennings' shack.

CHAPTER 11

PHIL COYNE AND HOBO JENNINGS HAD COME WEST together three years before. They were friends, not in the sense that they understood or needed each other but in the sense that they were used to each other. Each was a link between the other and his past.

Coyne didn't immediately understand why his horse balked near the front of Hobo Jennings, shack. Not until he had dismounted, irritably cursing the horse's stubbornness. Not until he had stumbled over Hobo's body and fallen on his hands and knees.

He got up, fumbling for a match.

"What's the matter?" Nate Goldsmith asked.

"There's someone here. Get down and help me get some light on him."

Goldsmith got off his horse and picked his way cautiously toward the sound of Phil Coyne's voice. He asked, "Who is it, Phil? Is it Hobo? Has he been hurt?"

"How the hell do I know?" Coyne snarled. "Get in here and help me find a lamp."

Goldsmith, probing ahead of him with an extended foot, encountered something soft and yielding, the body Coyne had said was here. He stepped over it. He could now see the square that marked the door, because Coyne had lighted a match inside the shack. He went in, fishing for a match of his own, and lighted it just inside the door. Coyne stumbled over a piece of firewood and cursed irritably again. "Where the hell is the lamp?"

Goldsmith found it and lighted it. He lowered the chimney, trimmed the wick, and carried the lamp outside. The instant the light touched the body in the yard he recognized Hobo. Coyne was already kneeling beside his friend. He said, "Take the lamp inside. Then come help me get him in."

Goldsmith took the lamp inside. He had known Hobo almost as well as Phil Coyne had. He went back and helped Phil carry Hobo into the shack.

Hobo was still alive, but his head was a pulpy mass of blood and matted hair. His chest rose and fell with his quick, shallow breathing. Coyne put his mouth close to Hobo's ear. "Hobo! Who done it, Hobo? Tell me who done it, hear?"

77

Hobo showed no sign that he had heard. Nate Goldsmith said, "He's hurt pretty bad. Somebody beat the hell out of him." He was looking around the room because he didn't want to look at the smashed top of Hobo's head. He saw the overturned woodbox, the scattered firewood. He asked, "Where'd he have the gold hidden, Phil. In the woodbox?"

"Uh huh. But it's sure as hell gone now."

"Who. . . ?"

Coyne turned his head savagely. "Who the hell do you think? Who killed McCurdy and his wife and boy? That sonofabitchin' Tom Condon, that's who. The sneakin', murderin' bastard!"

"But he didn't take McCurdy's gold."

"He didn't have time to look for it. Crawford and the others interrupted him."

Phil Coyne returned his attention to Hobo. He put his face close and asked, "It was Condon, wasn't it, Hobo? Condon done this to you, didn't he?"

Hobo groaned weakly. Coyne turned his head triumphantly. "See? Hobo said it *was* Condon!"

Nate said, "He didn't say nothing, Phil. He just groaned."

"Only because he's hurt too bad to talk."

Nate didn't argue the point. "He's hardly breathin'. Maybe I ought to get the Major and see if he can help."

Coyne shook his head. "Hobo's head's caved in. He ain't going to make it, Nate. There's nothin' the Major or anybody else can do."

"What are *you* going to do?"

"I'm going to Unionville. Condon ain't coming here with a posse. He just wants us to think he is. He's got a list of the men who were in on the raid and he's goin' down the list one by one. Lucy Wiley was killed on that

78

stage and Condon's out to get every man who was involved."

Goldsmith hesitated, finally admitting, "It makes sense, I guess."

"You're damn right it makes sense. And I ain't going to wait around town for Condon to show up with a posse, either. I'm going to Unionville. I'm going to kill Condon myself."

"You ain't got much chance alone."

Coyne was watching Hobo's chest. Nate Goldsmith turned his glance to it, but he couldn't see movement any more. He said, "Phil, he's dead. Hobo's dead."

Coyne laid his head down on Hobo's chest. He remained in that position for a long, long time. When he raised his head, his eyes were bleak. He nodded, got up, and started toward the door. Goldsmith asked, "You want me to go along with you? I kind of liked Hobo myself. I liked McCurdy, too That boy of McCurdy's reminded me of my David before he was taken by the smallpox years ago."

"You can go along if you want. But not if you're going to get in my way I'm going to cut Condon down. I'm not going to talk to him or anything. I'm just going to cut him down."

"That's all right with me. If we don't get him, he's sure as hell going to get all of us. He's already got two of us."

"All right then. Come on."

"How about Crawford? You going to tell him?"

"What for? He'd just give us a goddam argument."

Phil Coyne got to his feet. He stared down at Hobo for a moment. He shuddered slightly, then crossed the room and blew out the lamp. He went out the door and Nate followed him.

79

The pair swung to their horses. Nate heard a shout up the street from the direction of the hotel, but he didn't answer it. Phil reined his horse down into the bed of Grizzly Creek and splashed noisily across. Nate followed him.

For both of them, killing Tom Condon had become a matter of self-preservation. Condon was, they were convinced, working down the list, killing the stagecoach robbers one by one. The only way to stop him was to kill him before he killed any more of them.

Behind them now there were many shouts. A torch flared on the north bank of Grizzly Creek. The others had found Hobo Jennings' body. They would bury him, Goldsmith thought. And there were enough of them to take the gold across the pass. Hamidy and Fall could do that and if Crawford needed more than two he could send a couple of the other men. Or go himself.

Coyne was pushing his horse hard through the timber and drifted, unmelted snow, climbing a north-facing slope, heading straight toward Unionville. Nate Goldsmith wondered what time it was. He knew there was no use trying to see his watch, but he supposed that there were about four hours of darkness left. Enough to reach Unionville before the sky turned light.

But what if Condon hadn't returned to Unionville? He shook his head. There wasn't much chance that Condon would try for another of the men who had robbed the stage tonight. He had ninety pounds of gold in his saddlebags and his horse wouldn't be able to travel with any more weight than that. No, Condon would have headed straight for Unionville to get rid of the gold in his saddlebags. He'd plan on returning to Davistown again tomorrow night.

Coyne rode in almost sullen silence, his head sunk

80

forward onto his chest. Goldsmith didn't try to talk to him. But he tried to stay alert. There was a chance they would blunder into Condon out here in the empty reaches of the park. Not a good chance but a chance.

The air grew colder. Ice crunched beneath their horses' hooves. The hours dragged. Occasionally, where the ground was dry underfoot, Nate dismounted and walked, trying to keep warm.

He had not fought in the Confederate Army as so many of the others had. They had turned him down because he had consumption. As soon as he had been turned down, he left Kentucky and started west. He had intended to start a store and still intended to, but he had lost his money to bandits along the way. He'd come to Davistown from Denver hoping to make another stake mining gold, but it hadn't worked out that way. He'd been lucky to pan enough out of Grizzly Creek to eat.

Thinking about McCurdy and about Jennings got him to thinking about McCurdy's boy and that made him remember his own son, David, who had been dead ten years come May. Remembering David made him remember his wife, who had been gone almost as long.

He was a lonely man, but most of the men out here were lonely. Perhaps loneliness was the thing that bound men together out here in the goldfields of the West. Few of them had families. They learned to depend upon each other for companionship.

They also learned the meaning of loyalty. Even if he had not been involved in the stagecoach robbery with the others, Nate would have felt bound to try and avenge Hobo Jennings' death. Hobo had been his friend as well as Phil's.

As they traveled, the land became flatter. At last they struck the stage road between Ute Pass and Unionville.

Coyne followed it toward Unionville. Coyne knew the Union settlement better than anyone, Goldsmith thought. He had spent most of the winter there, waiting to bring news of the gold's departure to Crawford in Davistown.

Short of the town by half a mile, Goldsmith called out, "Where do you think he'll be, Phil? You got any idea?"

"He's got a little room off the main part of the jail. That's where he'll be. And that's where the gold will be."

"You going to try and get the gold back too?"

"I'm going to try. Them six sacks of gold will buy a lot of guns for the boys down South."

"What if Crawford's already sent the rest of the gold across the pass?"

"Then I'll take it and try to catch up with them."

They reached the edge of Unionville. There were no lights. The settlement was completely dark. Phil Coyne stopped his horse. He whispered, "Let's get down and lead the horses. We'll go up the alley behind the jail."

Goldsmith swung stiffly from his horse. He was shivering from the cold. He started to cough and put a hand over his mouth to muffle it. When he had finished coughing, he was soaked with clammy sweat. He followed Coyne across a vacant lot in which wild hay had grown up almost waist high, to an alley with two rutted wagon tracks. He glanced at the sky in the east, toward Ute Pass, and realized that he could see the high peaks silhouetted against the graying sky.

A square of light suddenly appeared ahead of them, slightly to the right. Phil Coyne stopped. "That's Condon's window, Nate."

"You think he's been asleep? He couldn't have had

more'n half an hour's start on us."

"Killin' a man and robbing him wouldn't bother Condon's sleep."

Nate said, "Maybe I'd feel the same way if the man I killed had helped murder the girl I was going to marry."

"It was an accident. Nobody meant to kill the girl."

Nate started to answer but changed his mind. Lucy Wiley was dead and no amount of argument would bring her back.

The square of light-suddenly dimmed as Condon picked up the lamp and carried it into the sheriff's office in the front part of the jail. Several moments later, both men smelled woodsmoke.

Nate asked, "Are we just going to wait here until he comes out?"

"You got a better idea?"

"We could shoot through the window. If we wait, there could be a lot of people around. We might not get the chance to shoot Condon without getting shot ourselves."

Coyne was silent for several minutes. At last he said, "All right. Maybe that is the best way of doing it. Tie your horse and come on."

Both men tied their horses. They crept silently through the high weeds and wild hay to the front of the jail. Here, Coyne stopped long enough to look carefully up and down. Nate, standing beside him, saw several more squares of light in windows along the street.

The sky was lighter in the east. In another ten minutes it would be light enough to see objects a hundred yards away. in twenty it would be light enough to see a rifle's sights.

Coyne said, "It's clear. Come on." He stepped carefully out onto the boardwalk in front of the jail.

Nate followed, careful to make no noise on the boards. He had his rifle gripped tightly in his hands. It was a single-shot weapon, but he also had a revolver in the holster at his side.

He could see Condon in the office, he was wearing pants, boots, and long underwear, but no shirt. The sheriff was standing at a washstand, stropping a razor. There was lather on his face.

Coyne whispered, "Get a bead on him. I'll tell you when to shoot."

Obediently Nate Goldsmith raised his gun. It was hard to see the sights because of the lack of light, but at this range an exact bead probably wasn't necessary.

A dozen feet away, Phil Coyne suddenly said, "Now!"

Nate fired. his gun roaring in unison with Coyne's. Glass shattered as the bullets smashed into the jail. A great cloud of smoke billowed from the muzzle of Nate's gun, momentarily obscuring his view. He dived aside, and ran for the horses, hearing Coyne's feet pounding along behind.

Back on the main street of the town, a door slammed open and a man's voice shouted something Nate could not make out. Coyne panted breathlessly, "We got him! We got the son-of-a-bitch, Nate! I saw him fall!"

CHAPTER 12

THE SHATTERING WINDOWS, THE ROAR OF THE TWO rifles so close that their noise threatened to burst his eardrums, the impact of the bullet, all these came as a complete surprise to Condon. Instinctively he flung his body to one side, falling, waiting for the second volley and knowing if it came he would have no chance to escape.

But no second volley came. Condon rolled halfway across the room, then leaped to his feet and charged for the door, snatching his gun from its holster as he did. He slammed back the bolt and flung open the door. Up the street somebody yelled at him, but he didn't take time to reply.

He rounded the corner of the jail at a limping run. Faintly, now, ahead of him, he could see the shapes of two horses tied to a fence in the alley beside the jail. He could see the running shapes of two men heading for them.

He raised his gun and sighted carefully in light that was barely strong enough to let him see his sights. He aimed low and was rewarded by the sight of one of the men going down. The other stopped to help him, got him to his feet, and the two disappeared behind the jail. Condon slowed warily, and was overtaken by several half dressed men carrying guns. "Where'd they go? Which way did they go?"

Condon said, "Behind the jail. Get hold of their horses first and tie them out in front of the jail. If they're afoot they can't get far."

The men plunged ahead. Condon yelled, "Wait a minute! Come back here!"

Nobody paid any attention to him. Like a pack of hounds baying on the hot trail of a wounded quarry, they ran ahead and disappeared behind the jail. Condon roared, "Damn it, I want them alive! You hear?"

But the men were gone and it was doubtful if they'd heard what he had said. A couple of them did lead the horses to Condon and hand him the reins before they whirled again and ran in the direction the other men had gone. Condon limped to the front of the jail and tied both horses to the rail. His whole thigh was soaked with blood from a wound in the fleshy part of his leg. It burned fiercely, but he knew it wasn't going to incapacitate him.

There was still lather on his face. He went into the office and snatched a ten-gauge double-barreled shotgun from the rack. He loaded it as swiftly as he could. A shotgun had authority a rifle or revolver couldn't have. Men who could face either a rifle or a pistol unflinchingly were afraid of a shotgun.

This gun wasn't for the two who had taken a shot at him. It was to cow the townsmen if a mob formed up to lynch the pair.

He snatched a towel and wiped his face. He crammed his hat on but didn't bother with a shirt. Carrying the shotgun, he went out into the cold dawn light.

Unionville wasn't big so it shouldn't take the townsmen long to run the dry-gulching pair to earth. Condon headed up Union Avenue in the direction both pursued and pursuers had disappeared.

Who the two were he couldn't guess. Nor could he guess their motive for trying to kill him the way they had. He supposed it was tied in with the theft of the gold from the stagecoach a couple of days before. Or it could possibly be tied in with the killing of McCurdy and his family. Perhaps the two were McCurdy's friends, seeking revenge for his death and for the deaths of his wife and son.

His leg began to ache ferociously. Blood had soaked the whole side of his pants. Near the wound it felt warm; farther away it was cold. He knew he ought to wrap something around it. He ought to check and make sure the bullet had gone cleanly through. But right now there wasn't time. If the dry-gulchers were caught and if they turned out to be Southerners from Grizzly Creek, they were likely to be shot. Or hanged.

There was another reason Condon kept running so recklessly up the street, limping ever more painfully as he did. He knew if he let his posse get out of control here in Unionville, he'd have no chance of controlling them once they reached Grizzly Creek later on today. They'd burn and sack the town and he wouldn't be able to hold them back.

A shot racketed to his right in the alley across the street from the hotel. He swerved and cut through a narrow passageway between two buildings. He barged into a pile of discarded, rusting tin cans at the end of the passageway and fell headlong. His leg twisted and he nearly lost consciousness from the pain.

He sat up, vision blurring, sweat springing from every pore. He gritted his teeth, fighting for full consciousness. There was more light now. The entire sky was gray. He could see the alley clearly through a gap in the slab fence that had been built back here. He saw two running figures go past. One of them was limping. He struggled to his feet.

A dozen or more townsmen streamed past the gap in the fence. Condon bawled, "God damn it, stop! I want those two alive!"

It was questionable if they heard. All of them were running as fast as possible. A couple were yelling crazily. Condon cursed disgustedly. If he wanted those two fugitives alive he was going to have to get to them before that crazy bunch of maniacs did.

He leaned against the wall until his head stopped

whirling, until spots stopped dancing before his eyes. He tried his leg to be sure it would hold his weight. Satisfied that it would, he limped back through the passageway to Union Avenue. If he thought it out, maybe he could anticipate where the fugitives would go.

Frowning he stared at the jail down the street. The two horses belonging to the fugitives were there at the rail where he had tied them a few minutes before. His frown disappeared. Of course. The thing uppermost in both the fugitives' minds would be horses, a means to escape the men hounding them through town.

They wouldn't try for their own horses in front of the jail. They'd figure that was too risky and it was. They'd go for the livery stable or for some private stable or corral if they happened across one as they fled.

Their path of flight had been south, toward the lower end of town. They'd probably go past the rear door of the livery barn.

Condon limped hurriedly down the street toward the big, log livery barn. He went in, stepping immediately to one side of the door so that he wouldn't be silhouetted against the light outside.

The place smelled of manure and horses and of the dry, dusty hay remaining in the loft. Faintly Condon heard a shout in the alley behind the place. He raised the shotgun warily.

A shot racketed suddenly near the rear of the barn. The bullet tore into the log wall a dozen feet above his head. All along the length of the barn, horses began to plunge and nicker in their stalls. Condon ducked into an empty stall as the second bullet whined past him and out through the open door. He yelled, "Now what? In about a minute those two shots will bring the mob in here and they'll cut the pair of you to bits."

Only silence answered his words. He waited a moment, then called, "Throw your guns out, then follow them with your hands above your heads."

Still no one answered him. Condon made his voice sound resigned. "All right. It's your damn funeral."

He heard the back door of the livery stable creak. He yelled, "It may already be too late, but if you want to live you'd better throw out your guns!"

A voice called, "All right! All right!" Two guns, tossed out from behind a wagon, thudded on the dirt floor of the livery barn. Condon shouted to the men out back, "They've surrendered! They're my prisoners! I don't want anybody shooting when they come out! If anybody does he'll answer to me!"

Nobody replied. Condon bawled, "Get out of here! Go out the back door the same way you came in! Go on now, damn you! I want these two men alive."

He raised up enough to see the long aisle between the stalls, enough to see the big door leading into the corral out back. He saw a man standing there, and shouted, "Damn it, get out! They've thrown down their guns and surrendered. Anybody that shoots them now is going to be jailed for murder."

A voice halfway down the long passageway called, "Condon, we may have surrendered, but we're not coming out. Not until that bunch clears out."

Condon got to his feet. He stepped into the open. He asked, "Is that you, Coyne?"

"It's me."

"Who's with you?"

"Goldsmith. Nate Goldsmith."

"What the hell are you doing here? Don't you know . . .?"

"We came after you for killing McCurdy and

Jennings."

"Jennings? Hell, I didn't even know Jennings was dead. When did that happen?"

"Last night. Four or five hours ago."

"Well, you came after the wrong man. I haven't left town all night."

There was a dead silence for a moment in the barn. A new voice yelled from the back door of the place, "He's telling you the truth, you Judas son-of-a-bitch! He hasn't been out of town."

Condon shouted, "You get out of here, Duckworth! I'm warning you, if you cut loose I'm going to shoot back at you!"

"Why, for God's sake? Coyne's the one that told them when the stage was leaving town. He lived here with us all winter just so's he could ride to Davistown and tell them when the coach was leaving with the gold."

"Charge him with it then. Charge him with murder if you want and hang him for it. But if you try shooting him while I'm taking him to jail, then you're the one that's going to hang."

Again there was silence in the livery stable, broken only when Condon called to Coyne, "I'm coming after you. Keep your hands above your heads. I'm feeling a little itchy about this and I wouldn't want to make any mistakes I'd be sorry for."

He walked slowly down the passageway, the shotgun held at ready across his chest. One hammer was thumbed back and his finger was curled lightly around the trigger.

At the rear of the stable, Duckworth shouted into the alley, "Come on in, damn you! If Condon takes them two to jail, they'll get off or get away. Let's save everybody a lot of trouble and kill 'em now. Let's hang 'em if that's what everybody wants. There's no damn use letting Condon put 'em in jail!"

A dozen voices shouted agreement, their words muffled by the thick walls but their tones unmistakable. Duckworth shouted something else at them, but Condon didn't catch what it was. He could see the two fugitives behind a wagon ahead of him, their hands raised above their heads, their faces white and scared. He said softly and urgently, "All right, hurry up! We haven't got much choice but to make a run for it. You go ahead and I'll follow you."

They hesitated briefly. Condon whispered urgently, "Come on! You're about out of time as it is!"

The two came out from behind the wagon and ran for the front door of the barn. Condon followed, glancing over his shoulder once. If Duckworth or any of the others shot at him, by God he was going to spray the back wall of the barn with buckshot.

Coyne and Goldsmith reached the wide front doors and plunged through them into the street. Condon was close behind.

Suddenly Coyne stopped and whirled. There was a little gun almost hidden in his hand. Smoke puffed from its muzzle. It made a sharp crack and the bullet creased a furrow in Condon's arm.

He was running and he slammed the shotgun barrel against the side of Coyne's head. Coyne staggered away and Condon seized the derringer and twisted it from his hand. He threw it angrily into the weeds beside the livery barn.

Coyne was standing with his head down now, swaying as if he was about to fall. Goldsmith's face was bloodless, almost gray.

Condon jammed the shotgun muzzle into Coyne's side. "Get over there to the jail, you dumb son-of-a-bitch. If you haven't got any better sense than to try killin' me now, by God you deserve to die!"

Goldsmith grabbed Coyne's arm and pulled him toward the jail. He opened the door and pushed Coyne inside. Condon followed. He prodded Coyne once with the shotgun muzzle as he herded the pair toward the cells at the rear.

Only when he had them inside and the cell door locked did he relax and push the hat back off his sweating forehead. He could feel a trembling of relief in his knees and in his arms. Maybe Coyne didn't realize how close death had been out there, but Condon did.

He returned to the front part of the jail, unloading the shotgun as he did. Things would be quiet now for a little while. But how in the hell could he leave his prisoners in Unionville without a guard while he led the posse to Davistown? He shook his head irritably because that was a question for which he had no answer, now.

CHAPTER 13

ALMOST IMMEDIATELY MEN BEGAN TO GATHER IN front of the jail. Condon went to the door. He saw Gene Lucas in the bunch and called, "Is there any window glass in town?"

Lucas shook his head. "Not that I know off."

"Then get some boards and nail them over these broken windows. Or some greased sheepskin."

Lucas nodded. He departed reluctantly, looking over

his shoulder.

Condon slammed the door irritably and shot the bolt. He went into the small room opening off the office, the room in which he slept. He took off his boots and blood-soaked pants and underwear. There was a bullet gouge on his left forearm. There was a hole in the fleshy part of his thigh. The hole was almost black, and for an inch around it the flesh was dark blue like a bruise. There was another hole four inches from the first where the bullet had come out. This hole was larger, surrounded by torn and shredded flesh. It made him sick at his stomach to look at it.

He got a clean shirt out of a dresser drawer. He ripped it into strips, and laid the strips carefully on the bed. He got a brown bottle of whiskey from the bottom dresser drawer and dumped some of it on the wound. He wiped it clean, then began carefully to wind bandages around his leg, sitting on the bed as he did.

There was sweat on his forehead and upper lip. Sweat ran in little rivulets down both sides of his face, which was twisted from the burning pain of the wound and almost gray despite the sweat. He wondered if he would be able to make the ride to Davistown today. He gritted his teeth and took a long drink from the bottle. Afterward he finished bandaging his leg and found a clean suit of flannel underwear and a clean pair of pants, which he got into with difficulty. He put on a shirt, rolling the sleeve above the bullet burn on his forearm. He bandaged that quickly, then strapped on his gun and hobbled out into the office again. The shotgun pellets smarted painfully, but he had no time to worry about them now.

The crowd was still milling around in front of the jail. Most of the men had horses and weapons and blankets and gunnysacks filled with food. But even those who were not going along today had guns. There was no yelling but there was a lot of ugly talk, some of which Condon could hear through the broken windows of the office. "How about that Judas son-of-a-bitch livin' here with us all winter just so's he could tell that bunch of rebel bastards when the stage was goin' outside with the gold?"

"Let's get him out of there and string him up!"

"Condon won't stand for it."

"The hell with Condon! Who's side is he on, anyway?"

Condon opened the door. His head was reeling and he felt as if he might collapse. He said, "Are you going to stand here all day blowing off your mouths about what you'd like to do to Coyne, or are you going with me to Davistown after the men who robbed the stage?"

"We're going with you! We can take care of Coyne when we get back."

"Then mount up and get started! I'll catch up."

Steadying himself on the doorjamb, he watched the confusion as they mounted their horses. Some of the animals bucked up and down the street to the accompaniment of high yells of excitement. Several guns were fired into the air. Condon frowned to himself. They weren't going to be easy to control. Even if he had been unhurt, he wouldn't have been sure he could manage it. Wounded and weak the way he was, he wasn't even sure he could ride as far as Davistown.

He closed the door, crossed to the small bedroom, got the bottle and took another drink. Then he went back to the cell where Coyne and Goldsmith were.

Goldsmith was sitting on a bench, staring gloomily at the floor. Coyne stood at the bars. He looked scared.

94

"Condon, you ain't going to leave us here while you take that posse to Davistown, are you?"

"What else would I do with you?"

"Who's going to guard us, and feed us?"

"I'll get someone to bring your meals."

Coyne stared at him, his eyes wide with fear. He said shrilly, "Jesus Christ, man, they're making lynch talk out there! You can't just ride off and leave us for those wolves!"

"You should have thought of that before you came here and took a shot at me." Condon stared angrily at Coyne. "You expect a hell of a lot if you expect me to be reasonable. There's a hole in my leg you could stick a gunbarrel through. I can hardly walk and I'm not even sure I can ride as far as Davistown. Why the hell should I care what happens to you while I'm gone?"

Goldsmith got up and came to the bars. His face was gray and lined with worry and with fear, but his eyes were calm. He said, "Because you're sheriff. Because you took an oath. You're supposed to uphold the law, not turn your back and let it be broken just because you're angry and in pain."

Condon glared at him. "You're pretty damned sanctimonious for someone who just got through trying to murder me."

Goldsmith smiled wearily, but he did not reply. He kept his glance steadily on Condon's face.

Condon turned and limped painfully back to the office. He slammed the door furiously. He walked to one of the smashed windows and stared out into the street.

Things had quieted somewhat since most of the men had left. He could see the last of the posse straggling out of town at the lower end of the street. He knew he had to make up his mind very soon. He didn't dare let them get too far ahead.

There still were more than a dozen men in front of the jail. He studied them speculatively, trying to decide how far they would go. Would they really break into the jail and take Coyne and Goldsmith out?

Probably not—not right away at least. They'd talk and they'd drink and they'd talk some more until they had worked their courage up to the required pitch. But there were a couple of men out there capable of inciting the others to lynch the prisoners and leading them in it.

He turned his head and stared, scowling, at the door leading to the cells where the two prisoners were. He knew suddenly that he couldn't leave them. If he did and they were lynched he'd never get over feeling responsible. He'd know he had killed them even though he'd been miles away when they were hanged. The chance that they would be alive when he returned was too slim to even bother considering.

But how was he going to get them out of here with that bunch hanging around in front? And what the hell was he going to do with them even if he did?

He cursed savagely beneath his breath. He knew Coyne and Goldsmith had been in on the stage robbery and the slaughter there. One of them might even have fired the shot that killed Lucy inside the stage. Both of them deserved to die. Why was he so damned concerned?

Goldsmith was probably right, he decided grudgingly. He was conditioned to doing things a certain way—the lawful way. That was why the violence at McCurdy's place had upset and embittered him so much. He'd wanted revenge for Lucy's death and for the other deaths at first, but he didn't want it anymore. All he

96

wanted now was to bring this business to a conclusion with as little bloodshed as possible. His frown deepened. It was like a forest fire driving along before a gale-sized wind. Maybe it could be stopped and maybe it could not. He only knew he had to try. He had no other alternative.

The first thing he had to do was to get Goldsmith and Coyne safely out of town. Then he had to hurry and catch up with the posse before they had covered too many miles.

Gene Lucas pushed the door open with his foot and came in. He was carrying a box of tools and some boards. Condon said, "I'll be back in a minute. Don't let any of those hotheads come in the jail."

"How the hell can I . . . ?" Lucas stopped because the sheriff had already gone.

Condon limped up the street. The sun seemed unbearably hot Spots danced before his eyes. His vision blurred and his head felt light. He knew what he was going to do, but he didn't know if he had the strength for it.

He passed Thomas Wiley's newspaper office and stopped suddenly. He needed help and he knew how much Wiley was against violence. Maybe the man would help him now.

He opened the door and went inside. Wiley was sitting at a desk, writing. Condon said, "I need help, Mr. Wiley. I need help or those two men down at the jail are going to be lynched."

Wiley frowned. "How can *I* help *you*?"

"Go over to Dickerson's place. He's got a lot of loose hay piled in that shed behind his house. Toss a match in it, wait until it catches, then run back here yelling fire. Can you do that?"

97

Wiley's face was pale, his eyes uncertain. Condon said, "It will save those two men's lives. Think of that instead of thinking that it's wrong to burn somebody else's property."

Wiley nodded reluctantly. Condon said, "Go on now. Hurry."

He limped back out to the boardwalk and headed down toward the jail. He could hear Lucas hammering as he boarded up the shattered windows. He went in and closed the door. He sat down wearily. He didn't have a horse saddled for himself and that mean he'd just have to let Coyne and Goldsmith go. After they had gone he'd go to the livery stable and saddle himself a horse.

Lucas had one window boarded up. The only light came through the other one. He said, "This'll be a dark place unless you leave the door open or light a lamp."

Condon shrugged. He was listening intently for Wiley's shout from the upper end of town.

Lucas went to the other window, measured it, and began to mark the boards to the desired length before sawing them. Suddenly he straightened. "What the hell was that?"

"What?"

"Somebody's yelling." Lucas went to the door and opened it. He stepped outside.

Condon could hear the shouting now. "Fire! Fire!" He crossed to the door and glanced uptown.

A column of smoke, already more than fifty feet high, billowed into the sky above Dickerson's shed. Lucas turned and glanced at him and Condon said, "Go on, Lucas. This can wait."

Lucas ran toward the smoke. The others who had been gathered in front of the jail hurried after him. Condon waited until they were well on their way before

98

he turned and went back to the cells where Coyne and Goldsmith were confined.

He unlocked the door. "Your horses are tied to the rail out front. Get on them and get out of town as fast as you can ride."

Both men looked at him suspiciously. Coyne asked, "What is this, some kind of goddam trap? The street's full of men just waiting to get their hands on us."

Condon shook his head. "Not anymore. I had a fire set uptown and they've all gone to put it out. But there's no time to stand here arguing."

Coyne and Goldsmith looked at each other. Coyne nodded slightly and the two bolted from the cell. Goldsmith was limping from the bullet wound Condon had inflicted on him earlier. Condon wondered how serious it was and realized that now he'd probably never know. He followed them out through the office and into the street, prepared to lay down a buckshot barrage if it turned out to be necessary. It was not. The street was deserted.

Coyne and Goldsmith untied their horses and mounted. Condon said, "I wouldn't head straight for Davistown or you might run into the posse that left here a few minutes ago."

Goldsmith looked down at him. He said, "We're getting better than we deserve."

Condon shook his head. "I'm not letting you off. I'll be coming after you."

Coyne reined his horse aside and drummed with his heels on the horse's sides. The horse broke into a gallop and Goldsmith's animal followed him.

Condon watched them until they were out of sight. Then he went back into the jail. He closed the door leading to the cells. He picked up the shotgun and went out into the street. Limping painfully, he crossed to the livery stable and went inside.

He leaned the shotgun against the doorjamb and walked back to one of the stalls. He untied a brown gelding that he had ridden before and knew was both strong and sound. He led him to the tackroom at the front of the barn, found his saddle, blanket, and bridle, and put them on the horse. There was a boot for a rifle on his saddle and he shoved the shotgun into it. He wasn't likely to need a rifle this trip, but he sure as hell might need that scattergun.

He led the horse to the door of the livery barn. The column of smoke no longer rose into the air. Now there was only a haze rising and from that he knew the fire was under control.

He mounted the horse painfully and with difficulty. Holding the animal still with an inflexible hand on the reins, he tried to arrange his leg so that the pain would be bearable. He did not succeed. There seemed no way he could hold it that it didn't nearly blind him with pain.

Gritting his teeth angrily, he touched the horse's side with the heel of his good leg and rode out of town at a lope, taking the direction the posse had taken earlier.

He hung onto the saddle horn desperately, knowing he'd never catch the posse unless he held this pace. He just hoped he could retain his consciousness.

CHAPTER 14

COYNE DID NOT SLOW HIS HORSE UNTIL HALF A MILE separated the pair from the town of Unionville. His grin was shaky as he turned to look at Goldsmith. "Jesus!

For a while there I didn't think we were going to get out of that alive."

"Neither did I."

"How's the leg?"

"It's sore but it'll be all right. The bullet only gouged the skin."

Coyne proceeded, holding his horse at a trot. Goldsmith seemed content to follow a dozen yards behind. Coyne turned his head and called, "Looks like maybe Condon didn't kill Hobo after all. They claimed he didn't leave Unionville last night."

"Then who did?"

"Maybe somebody else from Unionville, but I'm beginning to doubt it. I think one of our own people did it for the gold."

Goldsmith didn't reply. His expression told Coyne he was thinking about the rest of the gold that had headed out across Ute Pass last night, perhaps with an inadequate guard because the two of them had gone off on their own to Unionville. Coyne said worriedly, "I think we'd better push these horses along as fast as we can. If we're not already too late to do any good."

He touched heels to his horse's sides and the animal broke into a steady, mile-eating lope. Goldsmith kept pace. Ahead, where Ute Pass crossed the Continental Divide, heavy black clouds hung over the peaks, obscuring them. A wind was stirring in the north, spreading the clouds down across the northern edges of the park. Coyne said, "Spring blizzard comin' on."

Goldsmith nodded, but he didn't speak. He just turned his collar up against the chill of the rising wind.

Crawford heard the excited shouting from the direction of Hobo Jennings' shack. He couldn't have said how he

101

knew it, but he did. Hobo Jennings was dead.

He began to run in the direction from which the shouts had come. First McCurdy, he thought angrily. Now Hobo. Condon was taking them one by one. He was striking them down like a stalking wolf. Damn him. Damn him to hell!

Hamidy and Fall and a couple of other men were inside Hobo's shack. A lamp smoked unheeded on the table. Hobo's body lay on the bed. The woodbox, beneath which Hobo had hidden the gold, was overturned. Otherwise there were no signs of a struggle or a search. Whoever had stolen the gold had either known exactly where it was or had watched while Hobo took it from its hiding place.

Crawford looked around at the group and asked, "Did you see anybody leave? Or hear anything?"

The men shook their heads.

Crawford said, "Well, the rest of the gold has got to go out tonight. We can look for Hobo's six sacks later. Where are Goldsmith and Coyne?"

"Haven't seen 'em, Major."

"The damn fools have probably gone to Unionville. Or else they're chasin' whoever killed Jennings." He stared at the men and at Hobo Jennings, muddy and limp on the rumpled bed. He said, "All right, cover him up. Get somebody to build a coffin for him. If one of you wants to sit with him that will be fine. But the rest of you come on. We've got to get that gold started across the pass. It feels like a storm's blowing up."

He stalked out into the muddy street. He was angry and irritated, but he was uneasy too. Jennings' death and the theft of the gold worried him because it didn't look like Condon's work. It looked like the work of somebody right here in Davistown, somebody who wanted the gold for himself.

The pack mules, three of them, were tied to the rail in front of the hotel. They wore packsaddles from which leather panniers hung, one on each side. A couple of saddle horses were also tied to the rail.

Crawford had earlier loaded the gold that had been in his possession, along with that found in McCurdy's shack. Now the other men who had been along on the raid came forth, and the heavy buckskin sacks were loaded into the panniers, which were then lashed down. Grub sacks and blankets were securely tied on top.

There was a cold, moisture-laden wind blowing down out of the north. Crawford realized that the pass could be pretty dangerous by the time the pack train got that far.

A couple of horsemen rode up and dismounted; Crawford stared at them irritably. Joe Danvers was one. Kiley Lootens was the other. Major Crawford barked, "I thought I told you to come at dawn! I don't want you hanging around here now."

Both Kiley and Joe were eyeing the packed mules and the two saddle animals. "Whatcha doin', sendin' out the gold?"

Crawford just stared coldly at the two, whose faces were barely visible in the faint light coming from the open door of the hotel Danvers said, "If you need more men to go along, I reckon Kiley and me could go."

"We have plenty of men for guards. Now you two go home and get some sleep. Come back at dawn. That's when the posse from Unionville will be arriving here."

Lootens started to speak, but Danvers nudged him to shut up. The two climbed silently onto their horses and rode away.

Frowning, Crawford watched them go. He didn't like either of them, so it was natural that he would suspect them of killing Hobo and taking his six sacks of gold. But that didn't mean they were guilty of doing it.

Still, it would be foolish now to send the gold across the pass with no more than two men to guard it along the way. What he'd better do was take two or three extra men and escort it himself at least as far as the foot of the pass. He and the others could still get back here by dawn. A full three hours of darkness yet remained.

He looked around at the men standing shivering in the street. Of the nine who had attacked the stage, three were dead. Two more, Coyne and Goldsmith, had disappeared and had probably gone to Unionville looking for Condon, whom they probably blamed for Jennings' death. That left only himself, Stebbins, Hamidy, and Fall, of the original nine.

Hamidy and Fall would have to take the gold. Crawford shouted suddenly, "Schwartz! Dittman! Bloom! Stebbins! You four go down to the livery barn and get saddle horses. I want you to go along with me and escort the mules a ways—at least as far as the foot of the pass. We can still be back by dawn."

The four moved away and disappeared into the darkness. Crawford walked to his own saddle horse, in whose capacious saddlebags he had brought the gold he'd had in his possession. He swung easily to the saddle. Hamidy untied one of the horses at the rail and Fall untied the other one. Crawford said, "Let's each of us take a mule. When we leave you on the pass, you can tie the mules together in a string, but right now let's play it safe. We don't know who killed Hobo yet. We don't even know how many were in on it."

Leading a mule, he rode across the street to the livery barn. The other two followed him. The three waited impatiently for several minutes until Schwartz, Dittman,

Stebbins, and Bloom came out of the livery barn. They mounted and Major Crawford led out.

There was an odd kind of elation in him suddenly. Except for the loss of Hobo's gold, the coup had been a tremendous success. All that remained now was to get the gold to the Confederacy, and there were men in Denver who would help do that.

The wind was colder now, and stronger too. The stars were all but obscured by thin clouds that seemed thicker toward the north. Crawford thought he felt a flake of snow, but he could not be sure.

He led the column straight east toward the Ute Pass road. He turned up the collar of his coat and huddled down to help protect his face and ears. Soon, he thought, he'd be able to go back home again. Once they knew what he had done, the government of the Confederacy would summon him. They'd want him in some position of trust and responsibility. Maybe he couldn't fight with only one arm, but there were other things that he could do. He was wasted out here in this desolate wilderness.

The gold-laden mule plodded along behind him, sometimes pulling aside, trying to get his rump to the wind. Back farther, Crawford could see the others coming along laboriously.

The miles dragged and so did the time. More flakes of snow struck Major Crawford's face. The peaks loomed ahead, and at last the cavalcade struck the road leading to the pass.

Traveling in the road was faster than traveling across country. Crawford now lifted his horse to a trot, balancing himself in the stirrups lightly against the rough motion of the horse's gait. The panniers hanging from the packsaddle banged against the pack mule's sides.

Crawford was trying to plan his strategy for the battle that would be fought at dawn. The men of Davistown were certain to be outnumbered. That meant he would have to even the odds some way. He'd have to plan some kind of ambush for the force from Unionville.

Frowning, he realized that Condon would be on the lookout for an ambush. He'd run into one before, had spotted it and turned aside. Therefore the ambush would have to be planned to take into account Condon's expectations. Crawford began to smile coldly to himself.

What he needed was an ambush Condon could see— and another he could not. Avoiding the first, he'd run headlong into the second one.

He began to smile to himself. He raised his head and stared at the sky. If this storm materialized, if the snow thickened sufficiently, then ambushing Condon's column would be made much easier.

The road stretched away endlessly, but at last they reached the point where it began to climb steeply toward the pass. Crawford raised an arm and halted his horse and the mule he was trailing behind.

The others also stopped. The air was now filled with fine snowflakes, driven almost horizontally on the wind. Crawford shouted. "One of you come get this mule! Then tie them in a string, halter ropes to tails, so that one man can lead all three!"

A hunched figure came toward him and took the mule's halter rope from him. He could see figures moving around in the darkness, showing black against the ground which now was white with its light covering of snow. At last the three mules were tied together, and Hamidy took the halter rope. Crawford rode to him and raised his hand in a casual salute. "Good luck!" he shouted. "Go to a man named Wilhite in the Red Horse

Saloon at Ferry Street and McGee. He'll give you the help you need, and whatever men you need."

Hamidy raised a hand to show that he had heard. Leading the mules he went on up the road toward Ute Pass. Fall, hunched against the storm, followed along behind.

Crawford and the other four watched until they disappeared into the swirling cloud of snow. Then Crawford yelled, "Let's go back!" and turned his horse toward the floor of the park and Davistown.

Behind came the other four, trotting their horses on the snow-slicked road. The sound of the wind seemed to mount to a sullen scream. Crawford, hunching down into the collar of his coat, smiled slightly in anticipation of the action with the force from Unionville.

It would be a more decisive battle than many a bloodier one fought in the Confederate states. Engaging the force from Unionville would prevent their pursuit of the gold across the pass. Winning would mean that the gold claims at Unionville could be seized by the men from Davistown. More gold could be sent to the Confederacy. Despite the cold, Crawford's feeling of satisfaction increased. What he had begun with the attack on the stagecoach from Unionville was about to be finished with the battle to be fought at dawn.

CHAPTER 15

JOE DANVERS AND KILEY LOOTENS RODE ONLY FAR enough to be lost to Crawford's sight in the dark. Then Danvers reined in his horse. He said softly, "They're taking it out tonight. By day after tomorrow it will be in Denver and out of our reach."

Kiley growled, "It's out of our reach right now. Crawford's going to send enough men with it to see that it gets through."

"Maybe not. He knows he's going to have to fight Condon and the bunch from Unionville tomorrow. He knows he's going to be outnumbered and that he'll need every man he can get."

"So?"

"So he'll probably just send a heavy guard as far as the foot of the pass. From there he'll send the pack mules on with a couple or three men, and the rest will come back here."

Kiley said, "I don't know. . . Joe, we've got enough. We've got over twenty thousand dollars in gold. Think of it. Ten thousand apiece. That's more money than a man can make in fifteen years of work. Let's settle for it, Joe. Let's take it and get out and leave the rest alone."

Danvers growled, "We could have ten times that much We could live like kings. Just one night's work, Kiley, and we could spend the rest of our lives like kings. Besides, stopping that gold is the patriotic thing to do."

"Patriotic? For a Southerner?"

Danvers chuckled. "Who said I was a Southerner? For that much gold I'm a Northerner. I'm as much of an abolitionist as old John Brown."

Kiley didn't laugh. Danvers said, "We got to make up our minds. There ain't much time."

"How do you want to do it? You got a plan?"

"Not exactly. But if we left right now and went straight to Ute Pass, we could be waiting when they got there with the gold. We don't have to try for it if there are too many men guarding it. But if there's only two or three we can pick them off."

"I don't know. . . Hell, Joe, I'm getting scared. What if—"

Danvers interrupted, "Think of it, Kiley. Anything you want. You could have anything in the whole goddam world you took a fancy to."

Kiley did not reply. Danvers' voice was irritated when he spoke again. "You just think about something else while you're thinking about that. We've already killed a man and stolen twenty thousand in gold. Will we hang any higher for killing two or three more and stealing ten times that much?"

Kiley's voice was thin. "All right. All right!"

"Let's get going, then."

"Joe?"

"What is it now?"

"If we're not back here by dawn . . . Crawford will know that it was us."

"Then we'd better be back by dawn. And that means we'd better get moving now."

"We'll leave tracks. . . "

"Oh for Christ's sake! Do you want a guarantee that we'll get away with it? There's a storm coming up and it will probably snow. The snow will hide any tracks we make."

Danvers rode out, heading for the upper end of the street. From here he cut straight across country heading for Ute Pass. Kiley followed him silently, lifting his horse to a matching gait when Danvers spurred his to a lope.

Not knowing whether Major Crawford had left Davistown yet with the gold train or not, Danvers kept his horse at a steady gallop, seldom stopping to rest. Even after he reached the Ute Pass road he kept going and did not slacken pace. But short of the foot of the pass by about a mile, he drew in his horse and dismounted.

Bending low, he quested back and forth across the road, staring at the ground. He straightened, muttering, "There are tracks but I'm damned if I can make them out."

The wind was stronger even than before. It blew straight out of the north and it carried an occasional stinging flake of snow. Danvers shrugged as he climbed back on his horse. "They look like old tracks, but there's not enough light to tell. Anyhow, I guess if we're behind the mules, we ain't going to catch 'em anyway."

Kiley Lootens made no reply. He rode hunched down into his sheepskin coat, looking like a lump atop his horse. Danvers kicked his horse and continued until the road began to climb steeply in a series of switchbacks toward the pass. Here he paused once more, this time to rest the horses before beginning the climb.

Now it was snowing hard. His face was wet with melted snow. There was a thick coating of it on his clothes, and the damp air carried a penetrating chill he had not noticed earlier.

He gave the horses ten minutes' rest, then turned his mount and began the long climb to the summit of the pass. He was trying to remember the road from the few times he had been over it. He wanted to locate a spot, close to the road, where rocks were thick enough to make an ambush possible. He wanted shelter from the wind and cold during the time they would have to wait. If possible he wanted to station Kiley on one side of the road, himself on the other, so that they could cut loose on the men with the mule train from two directions simultaneously.

At the top of the first long ridge, Danvers halted the horses for a second time to rest. Holding his horse still and raising a hand to Kiley by way of telling him to do the same, Danvers listened intently. He thought he had heard a sound from below, but he was not altogether sure. Then, on a shifting gust of wind, he plainly heard a shout.

He grinned at Kiley, even though he knew the man couldn't see the grin. He waved an arm forward up the narrow, rocky road.

It went over another crest, wound a tortuous path along a steep hillside, and dropped down into a shallow basin before it began its final, steep ascent.

Snow here was already several inches deep, but tracks drifted over minutes after they were made. Suddenly Danvers saw the spot.

Midway across the shallow basin the road went through a tall jumble of jagged granite rocks which perhaps thousands of years before had broken off from the rocky peaks north of the road and tumbled down.

Danvers rode close to Lootens and yelled. "This is it! Tie your horse back of those rocks over there, get your rifle off the saddle, and wait. When you hear me shoot, open up. And be damn sure you knock a man out of the saddle when you do. They ought to show up good against all this snow if they ain't too far away. But don't shoot unless I do. All right?"

Kiley nodded vigorously.

Danvers yelled, "Soon as we've got 'em all, get your horse and go after the mules. We don't want them stampeding and getting lost in this damned snow!"

Again Kiley nodded vigorously. Danvers watched

111

him ride into the jumble of rocks across the road and disappear.

He withdrew into the rocks on his side of the road. He got off his horse and led him back until he found a place where he could tie him out of sight. Carrying his rifle, he returned, looking for a place he could hide.

He found one behind a rock about four feet high. It was just high enough so that he could kneel behind it and rest his rifle on its top. It even had a little V-shaped groove that suited the purpose admirably.

He strained his eyes, staring into the blackness and the whirling clouds of snow. Snow blew straight into his face, for he was facing north. It clung to his face and melted, and ran down across it, some even going into his eyes. Angrily he brushed it away with a hand that was almost numb.

He heard another faint shout from the direction they had come. He jacked a cartridge into the rifle and lowered his cheek to its stock.

Peering at the road over the rifle sight, he realized how chancy it was going to be, trying to hit anything in the dark. But there wasn't any help for it. It wasn't going to get any lighter for a couple of hours at least. By then the mules and gold would be half a dozen miles away.

A black shape came into sight on the road, materializing with what seemed like agonizing slowness into a horse with a man riding it. Behind the horse other shapes were visible, probably the mules.

He got as careful a bead on the man as possible, but he didn't shoot. Kiley was farther along the road. If he shot the first man in line, there wouldn't be anything for Kiley to shoot at. The man or men bringing up the rear could circle around these granite rocks.

112

His finger was tight on the trigger as the man rode past less than fifteen feet away. Three mules followed him. He was leading the first, but the second was tied to the tail of the first and the third to the tail of the second. The man leading the mules was almost out of sight before the second man came into view.

Again Danvers got as careful a bead as possible. He turned his head and glanced in the direction the first man had gone. He had disappeared in the snow and so had the first of the mules. If he didn't shoot now, the first man would have gone beyond Kiley's hiding place.

He'd have to risk the possibility that there were other men behind this second one. He didn't have any other choice.

He squeezed the trigger and felt the gun kick against his shoulder. Black powdersmoke rolled from the muzzle of the gun, for an instant obscuring the man at whom he had shot.

The wind cleared it away immediately and Danvers was gratified to see the man falling backward across the horse's rump. He fell from the saddle, but he did not fall clear. One foot hung in the stirrup and the horse, terrified by the sudden and unexpected roar of the gun almost in his ears, bolted past the uneasy mules, dragging his rider through the jagged snow-covered rocks.

Without waiting, Danvers leaped to his feet. Jacking another cartridge into the gun, he sprinted back along the road, expecting at least one other man.

Behind him, muffled by the driving snow, its sound almost snatched away by the wind, another rifle cracked. And again it cracked.

Danvers ran for about a hundred yards without encountering anyone. Turning then, he ran back swiftly, sweating, panting from the exertion of the run and perhaps from excitement too.

He reached the rock behind which he had hidden earlier. Without slacking his pace, he swerved off the road and ran to where his horse was tied. The nervous animal tried to pull away, but Danvers cursed him savagely, got him under control, and mounted him.

Sinking heels into the horse's sides, he thundered back to the road, turned into it and rode in the direction the first horseman and the mules had gone. He didn't think of the possibility that Kiley would mistake him for one of the mule train guards.

His horse almost stumbled over another horse, prostrate on the road. Beside the horse lay the black, lumped shape of a man. Neither moved.

Danvers rode past, watching the ground now, looking for tracks in it.

Even in darkness, the mule tracks and those of Kiley Lootens' horse were plain. He rode at a steady gallop up the road for about a quarter of a mile, stopping suddenly when he saw the three mules ahead and a horseman just beyond.

Was it Kiley or was it Crawford's guard? He had no way of knowing and he didn't want to get shot by Kiley if it happened to be him. He yelled, "Kiley, it's me! It's me!"

Kiley rode toward him, leading the three heavily laden mules. Danvers felt a sudden surge of excitement. They had done it! They had brought it off! He and Kiley were millionaires!

It was suddenly more than he could stand. He raised his face to the black, snowy sky and yelled incoherently with joy. He laughed like a maniac. He slapped his horse's neck with his hat, trying without success to

114

make the weary animal buck.

Kiley was more subdued. He sat his horse quietly, as though awed by the wealth that now belonged to him.

Danvers roared, "All right, let's get back! We can cache this gold somewheres along the way and then just turn the damn mules loose."

Kiley did not reply. Leading the three mules he headed back down off the pass, with Joe Danvers following.

CHAPTER 16

GRITTING HIS TEETH AND HANGING DESPERATELY TO the saddle horn, Condon forced his horse into a steady lope as he headed out in the direction his posse had gone earlier. He stared at the black clouds spreading across the park from the high peaks to the north. It had probably been snowing on the peaks a good part of the night, he thought. It would certainly be snowing hard in Davistown before he and the posse got that far.

He didn't know whether he was glad or not. Snow would hide their approach, to be sure. But it would also hide any ambush the men of Davistown might have laid.

He shook his head sourly. Snow and the accompanying cold would make him even more miserable than he was right now, if that was possible. And the cold would probably intensify the pain in his wounded leg.

He caught himself wondering why he was trying so hard to avert a showdown fight between the Unionville force and the one in Davistown. As weak as he was and as sick, he ought to be in bed instead of out here riding, trying to catch up with a posse whose members probably didn't even want him to catch up. Furthermore, he wasn't sure he had the strength to ride as far as Davistown, let alone back again. And anyway, why did he care? The men who had robbed the stage had cold-bloodedly killed all the men guarding it and Lucy too. Why should he worry about their lives?

He supposed he cared because he knew they were not really killers or thieves. They had been caught up in a patriotic fervor just as scores of thousands of others had, back where the war was being fought. Crawford had stirred them up. Crawford was a hothead and troublemaker who couldn't or wouldn't forget that he had been a major of cavalry before he lost his arm. If the war really came to this isolated place it would be because Major Jefferson Crawford had brought it here.

Suddenly Condon knew he had to catch the posse whether they wanted him to or not. He had to keep them from clashing with the men from Davistown. Those who had attacked the stage should be caught and tried as criminals so that the people in Davistown who had not participated in the attack would not be dragged into it in the name of Crawford's twisted Southern patriotism.

Unconsciously he straightened in his saddle, gritting his teeth against the pain in his leg. He slashed the horse across the rump with the ends of the reins and the animal increased his speed, abandoning the steady, rocking lope for a run. Condon gripped the saddle horn so tightly with both hands that the knuckles turned white. His face was gray, but he was sweating too. He began to curse, softly and beneath his breath, at the weakness that threatened to rob him of consciousness.

How long he rode this way he could not have said. He

had periods when consciousness all but slipped away from him. Each time he was jolted back to full awareness by a sudden stab of pain in his wounded leg.

The tracks of the posse were plain and easily followed. He never strayed far from them, even when his consciousness slipped away. And at last he was rewarded by the sight of the men galloping along in a close-packed group half a mile ahead.

They did not slow their pace as he drew near, but he saw two or three look around. When he finally overtook them and pulled ahead, he drew his own hose into a gallop, then to a trot, and finally to a walk while the posse members reluctantly followed suit. Condon halted and turned his horse so that he was facing them. "What the hell are you trying to do, wear your horses out before you even get to Davistown? Or are you trying to stay ahead of me?" He glared at Holley and at Duckworth, who he knew were the firebrands in this group, the ones who had egged the others on.

Holley stared balefully back with his one good eye. The other was covered with a patch. Holley said, "We *were* trying to stay ahead of you. We want this conducted as a military expedition instead of as a sheriff's posse out to arrest criminals. This is war, Condon, and you damn well know it is. I'm taking charge. Sergeant, disarm him and take him into custody."

Duckworth kneed his horse toward Condon. He swung his rifle so that it centered on Condon's chest.

Deliberately, Condon removed the shotgun from the saddle boot. He didn't know whether Duckworth would fire or not, but he didn't think he would. Right now, with pain like a branding iron against his leg, he didn't care. He pointed the muzzle of the shotgun at

Duckworth and thumbed the hammer back. "Drop it or I'll blow your goddam head off!"

Duckworth looked at Holley questioningly. Holley snapped, "Sergeant, do as I ordered!"

"But Captain. . ."

Condon broke in, "Holley, if you don't think I'll shoot, you're making a big mistake. Duckworth gets the first barrel and you get the second one. I figure after that this posse will be ready to do what I tell them to."

Holley studied him carefully. Condon said between clenched teeth, "I killed McCurdy, and because of me his wife and boy are also dead. Do you think I'm going to hesitate about killing Duckworth? Or you? For refusing to carry out orders I have the right to give?"

Holley hesitated. Finally he let his shoulders slump. "All right, Sergeant, put away your gun. We can wait. From the looks of him he can't last long anyway."

Condon glared. "I'll outlast you." He swung his head and looked at the possemen. "In spite of what Holley said, this is a posse, nothing more. The only reason there are so many of you is because I don't want the people in Davistown to put up a fight. I want the gold and the men that stole it, and that's all I want. If anybody here doesn't like that or if they can't take orders from me, they can head back to Unionville right now."

Nobody left, but Condon had the uneasy feeling he would only remain in control as long as it suited Holley to let him do so. He said, "All right then, let's go on. We'll walk and trot these horses alternately so that they'll be some use to us when we arrive."

He let his horse move out at a steady walk. He didn't know how he was going to stand the roughness of a trot, but he knew he'd have to try. He had to remain conscious until this was over with. If he did not, Holley

118

would see to it that Davistown was sacked and burned and all its people killed.

The wind was blowing stronger now and low-scudding black clouds hid the sky and sun. A few stray flakes drove along horizontally on the wind. Ahead, snow was like a curtain moving across the land, obscuring everything behind it.

Holley stood in his stirrups and waved his rifle forward. "Let's get going, men! If we don't, we won't get there at all! That looks like one hell of a storm!"

A few of the men touched heels to their horse's sides. Tom Condon turned his head and roared, "Hold it! You're not taking your orders from him!"

The men slowed their horses and afterward held them at a walk, looking uneasily from Condon's face to Holley's. Their respect for law and Holley's lack of official standing in the community was holding them in check. But if he showed weakness or lost consciousness—they'd be gone at once.

The curtain of snow was now less than a quarter mile away. Condon rode steadily, watching the inexorable way it rolled across the land. He was thinking that if it was thick enough, and wet enough, and cold enough, it might enable him to delay this posse and perhaps prevent the clash that had earlier seemed inevitable.

Then they were in the storm. At first it consisted of stinging pellets of sleet that made them duck their faces into the collars of their coats and pull their hat brims down. The horses' tails whipped out like banners in the wind and they tried to turn south and put their rumps to the icy, driving wind.

Then the snow came, close on the heels of the sleet that had already whitened the ground. It was a fine, swirling cloud, so thick it sometimes nearly obscured the man riding immediately to Condon's right. Except for that man, he might have been riding alone in a swirling void of screaming white. The temperature must have dropped fifteen or twenty degrees in a couple of minutes, Condon thought.

It would be useless to shout at the men, he realized. Useless to try and communicate with them. All they could do was go on, staying close together in a group so that none would be separated from the others and lost, perhaps to perish in the cold.

Suddenly, in spite of the cold and the pain in his leg, Condon began to smile grimly. The storm was exactly what he needed. There wasn't a man here who could keep his bearings in a blinding blizzard like this one was. He was in control again. There wasn't going to be any battle with the men of Davistown today. There wasn't going to be anything. He would lead the posse around aimlessly until he had worn them out. Then he'd take them back to Unionville. By the time the storm had cleared, perhaps some sanity would have returned to them.

All he had to do now was fight the weakness and the pain brought on by his wound. All he had to do was keep his head.

He clenched his jaws and closed his mind against the pain. He began to bear right very gradually until the wind was on his left and a little bit behind. On this course they would miss Davistown by a dozen miles.

The ride became a steady monotony of bitter cold and blowing snow. The men rode silently, concentrating on keeping together and keeping warm. A fight with anyone under conditions like these would be suicide, Condon thought. In this blizzard a man wouldn't even know his friends from his foes.

The hours passed. Condon tried to remain north of the Ute Pass road because he knew that if he crossed it, the men would realize they had been led astray. He'd have to turn back soon, he thought, but when he did he figured he could make them believe he had simply become lost in the storm.

Landmarks appeared that he recognized. Finally he raised an arm. He pointed to a low peak rising alone from the floor of the park. He shouted, "I guess I got lost. That's Mount Logan and it's ten miles south of Davistown. We'll have to go back, but the road is only about a mile and a half south of here."

There wasn't any grumbling. Even Holley seemed content to give up and go back to Unionville.

Condon turned and led them south toward the road. Suddenly, directly ahead of him and moving at right angles to his course, he saw blurs of movement that could only have been horses traveling in single file.

He gave no sign that he had seen anything, believing he had blundered into a party of men from Davistown. But as he continued, something about what he had seen bothered him, some faintly remembered impression that for the moment evaded him.

Suddenly he knew what it had been. Not all the shapes he had seen so vaguely in the storm had been carrying men upon their backs. Some had apparently been pack animals. . .

He raised an arm and the posse halted behind him, closing up, milling as they did. Over the shriek of the wind he yelled, "Pack mules! That way! Come on!"

His leg seemed to have turned numb. The pain had been growing less for some time now, almost as though a drug had been injected into his veins. He knew it was the cold that had deadened the pain and while he feared

121

freezing in the leg he was momentarily grateful for the lessening of the pain.

He kicked his horse into sluggish movement with his good foot. The horse would do no more than trot, but since the other animals had been moving at a slow walk, he figured that would be speed enough. He headed in the direction the pack mules and riders had disappeared, his posse fanned out behind him.

They rode this way for what seemed a long, long time. Condon was about to order them to spread out in a line so as to cover more ground when he spotted something dark ahead of him.

At almost the same instant a gun flared dimly in the storm ahead. Something struck the horse of the man next to him and the animal went down, kicking and floundering helplessly in snow that was now over six inches deep.

Condon turned his head and yelled, "Get up behind somebody else! Don't stay here!" Then he had gone on and the man had disappeared in the storm behind him.

He waited, his hand warming m his pocket until the last moment. When he could clearly see one of the riders ahead of him, he withdrew his revolver from its holster beneath his coat, raised it, took aim, and fired.

He was rewarded by seeing the saddle emptied, but he did not pause beside the fallen man. He went on, straining his eyes, trying to see through the blinding storm.

He passed three pack mules, standing disconsolately with their rumps to the storm. He kicked his horse into a gallop and an instant later overtook a second man.

This one also turned and fired, this time with a short handgun. The bullet missed and Condon yelled, "Throw down your gun!"

122

His reply was another muzzle flare. Deliberately, he raised his gun and took careful aim at the black, indistinct shape ahead.

Again he fired and again the saddle emptied instantly. He halted his horse this time beside the fallen man and waited until a handful of his possemen caught up with him.

"Load him up!" he yelled. "We'll take them back to town! I've got a hunch the gold is on those mules! Most of it at least!"

He remained still while the body was loaded onto the man's snow-encrusted horse. Then he rode out, heading for the road, while his posse, leading the pack mules and the horses of the two dead men, followed along obediently behind.

CHAPTER 17

IT WAS A NEARLY FROZEN, SILENT, UNUTTERABLY weary posse of fifty that returned to Unionville in mid-afternoon. They went into the Nugget Saloon, carrying the panniers from the three pack mules. Numbly they emptied the panniers onto the floor.

Condon, who had followed them in, limping painfully, stared at the stubby, heavy buckskin sacks of gold. He had counted them as they were dumped out of the panniers. Six sacks were missing but out of nearly sixty sacks, that was not too great a loss.

He was so near exhaustion he could scarcely hold up his head. He said, "Put the sacks in the safe here in the saloon. Detail a two-man shotgun guard and relieve them every four hours. Somebody get Mrs. Widemeier and send her down to the jail to take a look at my leg."

He hobbled toward the door. The men made way for him. Danger of a clash with the Southerners was over, he thought relievedly, at least for now. The gold had been recovered and that would take the edge off these men's will to fight. Besides, there wasn't a one of them who wasn't too tired to even think of fighting for a day or two.

Almost a foot of drifted snow lay in the street outside. It seemed more like winter snow than wet, spring snow. Condon limped across the street and opened the door of the jail. He lighted a lamp because the boarded-up windows didn't let in any light.

The office was like ice. Snow had drifted in through the cracks in the window boards. He built a fire in the stove with hands that would scarcely work, then spread his hands to the heat.

Before long the fire was roaring and Condon began to get warm. He removed his coat and hat. He stared longingly at the door of his tiny bedroom. He'd like to go in there and fall flat on his face. He'd like to sleep a week. But he didn't dare sleep at all unless he could get someone to stay here and wake him if there was need for it.

The two men they had surprised with the gold had been traveling away from Ute Pass instead of toward it. To Condon, that meant just one thing. They had stolen the gold for themselves and had probably been looking for some place to cache it.

Mrs. Widemeier came in, accompanied by Glen Braddock, who had been along with the posse. She was carrying her worn black bag. Mrs. Widemeier acted as midwife when there was need for it. She also dressed

124

bullet wounds and occasionally set broken bones. She was the closest thing to a doctor in Unionville.

A big, rawboned woman of fifty, she said crisply, "Get in there and take your pants off, Tom Condon. If you've got underwear over that wound, take your underwear off too. I'll be in as soon as I get some water hot."

She began rummaging around for a pan to heat water in. Condon didn't help because he knew she was competent to do it by herself. Instead he looked at Braddock, a stocky, gray-haired man who still had a Scottish accent when he talked. He said, "I've got to have a couple of hours sleep, but I don't dare go to sleep unless there's someone around to wake me if there's trouble. Will you stick around a while?"

"Sure, Tom. I'll stay."

"Can you stay awake?"

"Hell, I'm not sleepy. I'm just tired and cold. I'll have some food brought in and I'll be fine."

Condon nodded. He went into his little bedroom and sat down on the bed. He took off his boots and pants. His underwear was soaked with blood. He took out his knife and cut it all the way around his leg. He pulled the blood-soaked underwear leg down over his foot, clenching his teeth against the pain.

The wound had swelled considerably and was now puffy and red. It had bled copiously. Carrying a pan of water and some towels, Mrs. Widemeier came in and pulled a chair close to the bed. She put the pan of water down on it, then returned to get her bag. When she came back a second time she said, "Lay back, Sheriff. You'll be out cold before I'm through with you."

He grinned faintly, but he laid back as he had been told. He closed his eyes and seemed suddenly to be floating in a snowy void. He felt his leg being lifted, felt it gently lowered again. He smelled iodine and an instant later his leg was one great, fiery mass of pain. He opened his eyes to light that blinded him and then, suddenly, everything was dark.

Crawford and the others had ridden into Davistown at dawn. The people were ready, Crawford discovered. Women and boys and oldsters were patiently standing watch at windows all up and down the street. The men were in the saloon, their horses tied to the rail in front. Crawford went in and walked to the bar. He downed one drink, then turned and looked at the assembled men. "It'll be a damn miserable day," he said, "but by the time night comes there won't be any Union force left in the park. The gold claims at Unionville will be up for grabs."

"Who's goin' to get them claims, Major?"

Crawford looked at them. "The ones that distinguish themselves in the fighting are going to be first in line."

"Is the gold on its way over the pass?"

"It's on its way. Now let's go. We'll set up an ambush in the bed of Grizzly Creek."

They trooped out before him, talking and yelling excitedly. He mounted and led them out of town, down into the bed of Grizzly Creek, whose brushy banks afforded cover not only for the men but for their horses too. Grizzly Creek would also provide a quick route for changing position should Condon and the men from Unionville attack at an unexpected place.

Crawford picked four men and sent them out as scouts. Then he watched the others as they dismounted and tried to make themselves as comfortable as possible in the driving snow and biting wind. Some sought

126

shelter behind bushes and scrubby trees. Others hunkered down behind rocks. Still others grouped together, smoking and talking in quiet tones. All kept their weapons close at hand.

Crawford himself paced restlessly back and forth, slapping his boot-top and the leg of his pants with a willow switch that he had cut. He wished he had taken time to go home and put on his uniform; but it couldn't be helped now. At least, he thought, he had worn his Confederate cavalry hat, on the front of which was the insignia of the Army of the Confederate States of America.

The hours dragged past, but the storm did not abate. The scouts came in with nothing to report and Crawford relieved them and sent others out. At noon he passed the word that the men could build fires if they wished, because they were beginning to grumble that the force from Unionville probably wouldn't even come.

By mid-afternoon, Crawford decided they were right. Condon and the bunch from Unionville obviously did not intend to come today. He mounted his horse and rode up and down the bed of Grizzly Creek. "Put out your fires and mount! If they won't come to us, we'll go to them!"

"What if they come here after we're gone, Major? They'll burn the town!"

"If they're not here by now, they're not going to come. Mount up, and let's be on our way. We can reach there an hour before dark if we start right now. An hour will be enough for what we have to do. We'll spend the night in Unionville."

A few of the men grumbled, but most mounted cheerfully enough. Crawford was about to wave them out of the bed of Grizzly Creek when he heard one of the scouts shout faintly in the void of driving snow. He waited and saw the man come riding out of the snow and down into the bed of Grizzly Creek. He was followed by a man Crawford had never seen before.

The scout, Ira Stebbins, who had been along on the stagecoach raid, said excitedly, "I ran into this man on the road, Major. He just came over Ute Pass from Denver. I think you ought to hear what he has to say."

Crawford looked at the man, whose face was all but hidden in the collar of his coat and in the scarf he had used to cover his mouth and chin. The man yelled, "You Crawford? I got a message for you from Ben Hillman in Denver. It came by courier day before yesterday."

"What came? Get on with it, man!"

"It ain't good news, Major. General Lee has surrendered his army at Appomattox Court House. The war's over, sir."

Crawford felt as though someone had hit him in the pit of his stomach. Stunned, he stared at the man unbelievingly. "You're a liar! You're a dirty goddam liar, that's what you are!"

"No sir. I ain't no liar. It's the truth." The man held Crawford's glare with steady eyes. "There's more, Major. I found a couple of dead men up on Ute Pass. One of 'em had been dragged by a horse. They'd both been shot. I don't know who they were, but I figured maybe you might know."

Crawford shook his head unbelievingly. Suddenly he reached out and seized the man's coat front with his hand. He shook him with insane violence. "Liar! Liar! Tell me the truth or I'll shoot you where you stand!"

The man's face was pale and his eyes were scared, but he did not evade Crawford's glaring eyes. "I told you the truth. If you shoot men for telling the truth, then

128

I guess you're going to have to shoot me too."

Crawford released him and grabbed for his gun. Stebbins, big and slow-moving, caught his arm. "Maybe he is tellin' us the truth, Major. Maybe the war is over. And maybe somebody did get Hamidy and Fall up there on the pass."

"That would mean the gold was gone. It would mean that we had failed."

"The Confederacy can't use that gold, Major, if there ain't no Confederacy."

There was now a thick cluster of men around the major and the other two. Someone yelled, "If the war's over, then by God we'd just as well go on back home."

Another yelled agreement and another after that. They began to leave, going to their horses, mounting, keeping their eyes downcast as they pondered the enormity of the news they had just heard. Crawford yelled, "Wait! We don't know that what this man says is true! Lee hasn't surrendered! He wouldn't surrender! You can have my word for that!"

Nobody answered him. They looked at him, but they went on untying their horses and mounting them. They began to move out toward Davistown, a bunch of saddened, defeated men.

Within minutes, only Stebbins, Crawford, and the messenger were left. The messenger said uneasily, "If you're through with me, Major, I'm goin' on into town and get me somethin' to eat. I'm froze an' damn near starved."

Crawford nodded at him absently. "Go ahead."

He was staring at Stebbins. "You and me are the only two left. Hamidy's dead and so is Fall. So are Jennings and McCurdy and Stocker. Coyne and Goldsmith are probably dead too."

129

Stebbins was staring strangely at him. Almost as though he was talking to himself, Crawford said, "It isn't war anymore. We can say we did it for the Confederacy, but nobody will believe that now. We're just a couple of common criminals and we'll be hanged for what we've done."

Fear showed in Stebbins' eyes. He kept them steadily on the major as though counting on Crawford to come up with a way out for them. Crawford said, "You can do what you want, Stebbins, but I'm going to go through with it. I'm going to attack Unionville. I'll show those rabble that a Confederate cavalry man is worth fifty Northern civilians in a fight."

Stebbins glanced uneasily in the direction of Davistown. He turned his head and glanced at the major's face. He put up a hand and ran a finger around inside his collar, next to his throat.

With a little shrug he said, "All right, Major. The only other thing we can do is run, and I don't reckon we'd get very far."

Crawford turned his horse and climbed him out of the bed of Grizzly Creek. Stebbins followed, his expression fatalistic and without hope because he knew that only a madman would attack a town the size of Unionville. Only a madman would even consider it.

But there was still another reason Stebbins went along. He hadn't been sleeping well since the stagecoach attack. He kept seeing those dead men in his dreams. And that pretty girl, her face white and lifeless as she lay sprawled inside the overturned coach.

CHAPTER 18

IT WAS GROWING DARK WHEN CRAWFORD AND Stebbins arrived in Unionville. Crawford was still wearing the Confederate Army officer's hat, which was soaked and encrusted with frozen snow. He paused at the edge of town and Stebbins halted beside him. "What are you going to do, Major? There's nobody in the street to fight. You can't just charge up the street shooting into the air."

Crawford said grimly, "I'll bring them out."

"How?"

"We'll set fire to the livery stable. That ought to bring out every able-bodied man in town."

"It'll do that all right."

"Then let's get at it." He started to ride away, then stopped and returned to Stebbins. He put out his hand after removing the gauntlet from it. Stebbins took it a bit puzzledly. "What's this for?"

"You've been a good soldier, Stebbins; I just wanted to shake your hand."

Stebbins shook the hand self-consciously. The major's horse fidgeted. Stebbins said, "You figure we're going to get killed, don't you, sir?"

Crawford nodded. "If you don't want to stay with me, I won't order it."

Stebbins didn't seem to see anything ridiculous in the major's plan or in his words. He said, "I'll stay, sir. I guess I'll stay."

Crawford peered closely at his face. "Why? Why should you stay when you know it's almost certain death?"

131

Stebbins frowned. "Well, I guess for the Confederacy, Major."

"There is no Confederacy. Lee has surrendered."

Stebbins asked suddenly, "What do they do to a man for robbing a stagecoach and killing all the passengers and guards?"

"They hang him. Why?"

"Then maybe I'm staying with you because I'd rather be shot than hanged. And maybe because I feel bad about those people that we killed."

Crawford frowned. He dismounted. The sky was gray now with approaching dusk. The snow had abated and so had the wind. A few vagrant flakes still sifted softly out of the leaden sky. A star was visible through a break in the overcast. Crawford led the way up the street on foot, trailing his weary horse. Stebbins, who also had dismounted, followed him.

There were no people on the main street of Unionville. A few lamps winked through windows up and down the street. A few horses stood dejectedly at tie rails. The smell of woodsmoke was in the air and the smell of cooking meat.

Crawford went into the livery barn. He handed the reins of his horse to Stebbins. "Hold them. I'll climb up and set fire to the hay in the loft."

"What about those horses in the stalls?"

"Leave them."

"But. . ."

"Leave them. Don't worry, we won't let them burn. They may be of use to us later on."

Stebbins obediently held the horses. The major disappeared into the darkness. A few moments later Stebbins heard his footsteps in the hayloft overhead.

He waited. He was growing nervous and he was

getting scared. It was one thing to say you preferred getting shot to being hanged. But when it came to actually exposing yourself. . .

Light flared overhead as Crawford tossed a match into a dry pile of hay. The fire grew with frightening rapidity. Crawford called down, "Go to the door and yell fire. Keep yelling it until somebody hears."

Stebbins shuffled to the door of the barn, still leading the two horses. The horses had smelled the smoke and seen the flame. Highly agitated, they kept trying to pull away. Stebbins bawled, "Fire! Fire in the livery barn!"

He waited. Apparently no one had heard, so he shouted again. Still it seemed no one had heard. He turned his head and yelled, "Should I fire a couple of shots, Major? That might bring 'em out."

"Try it."

Stebbins withdrew his rifle from the saddle scabbard. He could hear the major coming across the manure-littered floor of the livery barn. He fired, waited almost a minute, then fired again. After that he bawled, "Fire! Fire in the livery barn."

Now, in the silence following, he could hear doors opening and closing, could hear shouts mingling up the street toward the center of the town. He said, "They're coming, Major. What are we going to do now?"

"Stand here and pick them off." There was a kind of wicked anticipation in Crawford's tight-drawn voice. "We just stand here and pick them off."

Looking out into the street, which was now almost wholly dark, Stebbins could see men running toward the livery barn. Some were fully dressed. Some wore coats over their underwear. Some were trying to finish dressing as they ran. Crawford raised his rifle and steadied it on the doorjamb of the livery barn.

Stebbins stared at him in horror. In spite of what he had told the major, he didn't want to see any more innocent people killed. He didn't want to kill anybody.

The major's gun cracked spitefully and out in the street, lighted faintly orange by the flames in the loft of the livery barn, a figure stumbled, then pitched limply forward to lie motionless in the snow.

Stebbins whirled. He released the reins of the major's horse and vaulted to the back of his own. Reins in one hand, rifle in the other, he suddenly released a high, thin yell and cracked the horse over the rump with the barrel of his gun.

The startled, frightened animal plunged out through the open doors of the livery barn. Stebbins leaned low over his neck, bringing the rifle up as though he meant to fire it but having no real intention of doing so. He had said this was better than hanging, but now he wasn't sure. He kept waiting for the bullets to strike, gritting his teeth angrily against the compulsion to whirl his horse and try, even now, to get away. He had helped to rob the stage and his gun had helped to kill the guards and passengers, but it had been useless because even as they died, the Confederacy had been dead for days. News of Lee's surrender at Appomattox must have taken a week or more to get here, perhaps longer even than that.

He saw the men of Unionville stop ahead of him. Startled by his sudden appearance and by the collapse of the man Major Crawford had shot, they stood in a ragged line stretching from one side of the street to the other. Most of them had buckets. Some had axes. Only a few had guns because they had come out to fight a fire, not a force of Confederate invaders from Davistown.

But the few guns now raised and barked. Flame

stabbed from their muzzles. A bullet struck Stebbins in the right shoulder and jerked him halfway around. The rifle dropped from his suddenly numbed and unfeeling hand. A second bullet took his horse in the throat, but before the horse could fall, a third struck Stebbins squarely in the chest.

The horse's head went down. Stebbins was driven back by the force of the bullet striking him. The horse somersaulted in the snow and Stebbins was catapulted forward to land ten feet in front of him. He landed on his head, but he didn't feel the bones snap in his neck. He was already dead.

In the doorway of the livery barn Crawford's rifle cracked again. Again a man went down.

Tom Condon's roaring voice suddenly filled the street from the open doorway of the jail, "Take cover, you fools! Take cover! Before any more of you get shot!"

They scattered, right and left. Again the rifle cracked in the door of the livery barn. A third man plunged forward to lie face down in the snow.

And then the street was clear. No longer did the mounting flames from the livery barn illuminate figures in the street.

Tom Condon stared from the doorway of the jail toward the livery barn. He stared at the four limp figures lying half buried in the deep, rutted snow. One of them began to crawl toward him as he watched and he called, "Stay still if you can. Stay still for a few minutes. If they see you moving, they might shoot you again."

The figure kept inching painfully toward him through the snow. He couldn't see the man's face because the fire was in back of him, but he could imagine how the pain must be twisting it. The man was dragging a smashed and useless leg behind him in the snow.

Condon gritted his teeth and cursed helplessly beneath his breath. Whoever was over there in the livery barn must be insane. The thing was burning over his head and it was only a matter of time before he'd be driven out into the street by the heat. The trouble was, neither he nor the people of Unionville could wait. The blizzard wind had kept building roofs free from snow; sparks from the barn, rising on a column of heated air, could carry the fire to every part of town. A dozen fires could break out minutes after the stable roof burned through. And if the townspeople couldn't come out into the open to fight those scattered fires, it would only be a matter of time until the whole town went up in names.

Condon now thought he could see the silhouette of a shadowy figure just inside the big stable doors. He had the fleeting impression of a wide-brimmed cavalry hat. . .

Crawford. That was who was in the barn. Major Jefferson Crawford, that pro-slave fanatic with the empty sleeve and the inability to forget the fact that he had been a major in the Confederate cavalry before he lost his arm.

He left the doorway zigzagging as he ran toward the opposite side of the street in an attempt to avoid any bullets that might be fired at him. His injured leg gave way and he sprawled face downward in the snow. He was up almost instantly, continuing his erratic progress across the street.

A muzzle flash lanced into the darkness from the right side of the stable door. He sprawled again, and as he rolled in the snow, trying to regain his feet, it flared a second time.

He reached the far side of the street and dived behind the protection of a building. He slammed into the wall and leaned there, panting, startled to discover that he was shaking violently. That was a hell of a way to have to find out how many marksmen were in the barn, but now he knew. Only Crawford. The major was all alone.

Flames were beginning to lick through the roof of the livery barn. By their light he could see smoke rising from the overheated planks and shingles of the roof.

He knew he was nearly out of time. In minutes that whole roof would burn through and send a column of sparks a hundred and fifty feet into the air. He had to get Crawford and he had to get him now.

There was only one way of doing it. He'd be killed instantly if he dared to try a frontal assault. The only other way was to go in through the rear door of the livery barn. And if the roof fell in while he was running from the rear door to the front, he'd be burned to death.

CHAPTER 19

As Condon limped along the alley toward the rear of the livery barn, he couldn't help feeling a certain grim satisfaction. It was necessary to eliminate Crawford to save the town, but there was going to be satisfaction in it too. Crawford had been responsible for the attack on the stagecoach and the theft of its cargo of gold. He'd had help, of course, but the idea had been his. He had been in command. His order had begun the slaughter of the guards and passengers. Whether by intent or accident, Crawford was directly responsible for Lucy's death.

He reached the corral at the rear of the livery barn. The air here was hot from the fire inside. Condon opened the corral gate and went directly to the rear stable door.

He opened it and stared down the long alleyway between the stalls. Horses were nickering shrilly with terror, rearing in their stalls trying to break their halter ropes, kicking at the sides. Condon hesitated only an instant, then plunged into the place. He tried to run but found that he could not. The pain in his leg was too intense.

He limped forward along the alleyway, trying to hold his breath so that he wouldn't have to breathe the smoky, overheated air. He reached the first stall in which there was a horse and started to go past.

The horse turned his head and looked at him. The animal's eyes were wide with terror and seemed to plead silently.

With a short curse, Condon crowded past the horse into the stall. The knot on the halter rope had pulled too tight to be untied. He reached for his pocketknife, opened it, and slashed the rope.

Instantly the horse backed out of the stall, whirled and galloped toward the front door of the stable. Condon went on, no longer hesitating, slashing halter ropes, releasing each horse he passed. One by one they thundered out the door.

Condon was breathing now, as shallowly as he could. His throat was raw from heat and smoke. His eyes burned and tears ran across his face. He bent double for a moment, coughing almost uncontrollably.

He straightened with an effort. He was wasting time, time that might mean the difference between life and death. There was a roar above his head, the roar of unchecked flames. Embers fell around him, starting little fires in the dry manure and hay on the stable floor.

He peered ahead, gun ready in his hand, trying to see Crawford at the door. But he couldn't see that far. The smoke was too thick, the heat too intense.

He went on, wondering if he would ever breathe clear, cold air again. He stumbled when his injured leg gave way and fell headlong. A glowing ember on the floor started his pants to smoldering and he took a precious moment to beat it out with his hand.

He discovered that the air close to the floor was breathable. Cold air seemed to be flowing in one of the doors like water and like water it remained close to the floor. If he crawled the remainder of the way. . .

Breathing again almost normally, he crawled laboriously on toward the front door where Crawford was. His head felt light. Bright lights flashed before his eyes. He was nearly overcome by smoke, he thought, or by lack of air, or by heat, or by a combination of the three. He was nearly out of time.

Suddenly, the roof of the stable collapsed with a deafening roar. Sparks showered down through every opening in the loft. In places the weight of the blazing rafters collapsed the floor of the loft.

Condon was showered with sparks. He rolled to extinguish half a dozen fires started by them in his clothes. No air now remained on the floor of the livery barn. He got up, choking, and plunged toward the door again.

Suddenly, ahead, he saw Crawford's shadowy shape. The man held the halter rope of a terrified horse in his hand, a shortened halter rope, one that Condon had cut. He seemed wholly occupied with trying to control and mount the horse. With only one arm, it seemed doubtful if he would manage it.

Condon roared, "Crawford! Hold it!"

Crawford jerked his head around. The crown of his hat was smoldering but the Confederate Army insignia on the front of it caught the yellow light of the flames and threw it back.

Condon's revolver was in his hand. He yelled over the roar of the flames, "Let go of the horse! Don't try to grab a gun! You're under arrest!"

Crawford hesitated between trying to vault to the horse's back and releasing him and grabbing his holstered gun. Condon couldn't guess what decided him, but suddenly Crawford released the horse. The animal plunged away, to disappear into the night. Crawford grabbed for his gun.

Condon yelled, "No! I'll. . . " Then instinct took control of him. The hammer of his revolver came back, the muzzle came into line, and his finger tightened on the trigger.

His instant's hesitation had given Crawford time to get his gun clear. Its muzzle was also up in line, its hammer also back.

Both guns fired almost simultaneously. Crawford was driven bodily out through the stable doors. He fell on his back in the mud just outside of them. On his back he tried to raise the gun and fire it again.

Condon fired a second time. The bullet, directed at Crawford's chest, took him in the throat instead. There was an instantaneous gush of scarlet blood that drenched the front of him. His arm dropped limply to the ground and the gun slipped from his fingers. He lay completely still.

Condon limped wearily and painfully out past him into the street. From all directions men came now with axes and buckets, with shovels and water-soaked gunnysacks to be used in beating out small fires started by flying sparks.

Condon crossed the street to the jail. He did not glance at any of the bodies lying in the street. He'd seen enough dead men to last him a long, long time.

But it was over now. It was over and while men had been killed, the war had not succeeded in coming to this Colorado mountain valley, to Davistown and Unionville.

He sat down wearily in his chair and stared at the flickering lamp. He had succeeded, he supposed. But all he could see in his thoughts was Lucy Wiley's face. And all he could feel was an empty sense of loss.

We hope that you enjoyed reading this
Sagebrush Large Print Western.
If you would like to read more Sagebrush titles,
ask your librarian or contact the Publishers:

United States and Canada

Thomas T. Beeler, *Publisher*
Post Office Box 659
Hampton Falls, New Hampshire 03844-0659
(800) 251-8726

United Kingdom, Eire, and
the Republic of South Africa

Isis Publishing Ltd
7 Centremead
Osney Mead
Oxford OX2 0ES England
(01865) 250333

Australia and New Zealand

Australian Large Print Audio & Video P/L
17 Mohr Street
Tullamarine, Victoria, 3043, Australia
1 800 335 364